Not Your Abuelita's Folktales

Aaren,

Thank you for being a great student and coming to support my writing dreams!

María J. Estrada

Copyright © 2019
María J. Estrada

First edition published by Amazon.

ISBN: 9781071410158

Cover Design: Brett Jelínek
Cover Art: Jenny Moy Croitoru

Printed in the United States of America.

Contents

Foreword

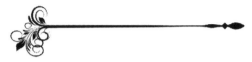

I wanted to say a few words on my use of Spanish before you immersed yourself into these modernized, supernatural folktales.

When I first thought about how to deal with the Spanish, I was going to add a glossary. However, as a reader, I find going back and forth from glossaries to stories to be tedious. Also, I am not partial to translating the Spanish, directly after the Spanish use because as a bilingual reader, I am reading the same words twice. I think this is true for a lot of multilingual readers.

Thus, I decided to be rebellious and took a page from Pulitzer Prize winner, Junot Diaz. I didn't differentiate the Spanish by italicizing it because for readers who read more than one language, there is none. One language is not more important than the other, and I wanted to reflect that in my stories.

Instead, I set the Spanish inside short dashes, as you would see it in traditional Spanish dialogue, especially with full sentences. For non-Spanish readers, I footnoted essential segments, unless the meaning was clear from the context of the passage.

Thank you for being understanding, as my usage of the Spanish reflects the reality of people living along the U.S.-Mexico border.

¡Disfrútenlo!

The Extravagant Stranger

S he smiled coquettishly at the dead miller's son. Rosa Maria couldn't remember his first name, but she lingered on his face. He blushed, and she swung her hips one last time as she entered the local mill. The smell of corn filled her lungs; she wasn't partial to that odor. Still, her smile widened, when she spied Mr. Sanchez working alone. He was sweating, his simple shirt clinging to his thick muscles.

He was young, five years older than Rosa Maria, and he had inherited his father's maize mill at the young age of 23. He averted her gaze.

"How many kilos?" he mumbled.

She paused, forcing him to look up. "Five, please." She handed the large bowl over, which he filled with a mixture of ground maize, lime, and water.

She cocked her head and asked sweetly, "Don't you need to use the scale?"

He grew irritated his upper lip curling upward. "You doubt me, señorita?"

He grabbed the bowl and dumped the meal into the scale. It read five kilos. He put the mixture back into her bowl and handed to her, pushing her away in the process.

"Thank you so very much." She said, "I pray for you and your family every day, for the repose of your dear father."

He turned his back and added more water to the corn as he began to grind another large batch. She turned walking provocatively, until her neighbor Elena marched in with a large bucket.

"Hello, Rosa Maria." She smiled.

Rosa Maria tried not to grimace. The old woman's two front teeth were missing. Rosa wondered why in God's name the woman just didn't go to a dentist in Durango. After all, in 1960, there were plenty of medical advances, or so she thought. Still, she prayed with all of her might not to look that awful when she grew old. In fact, she would give *anything* to never grow old.

The shop window shutters opened letting in a rush of cold air.

The old woman crossed herself and advised, "Get home. The wind is picking up, and you don't want to catch a cold."

On a search for sweets, Rosa Maria walked to the local shop. Ricardo was working there, and he always gave her a few hard candies for a kiss on the cheek.

She continued home, hoping to catch another young man's attention. Instead she spied a beggar on the street, an abandoned old man most people ignored. She handed him a couple of candies and one last peso she hid in her cleavage.

He smiled at her and gave her a heartfelt blessing, "May the hand of God rest on you." Rosa Maria squeezed his shoulders and wished she owned the means to find him shelter.

On the way down the cobbled street, the hairs on the back of her neck stood. Someone was admiring her rear end. She looked back towards the mill, which was just a few blocks away. But it was not Mr. Sanchez.

His loss, she thought.

FROM THE ROOFTOP, he looked down at her. She was an exquisite specimen, his Rosa Maria. Her impertinence and arrogance were alluring. He loved how she swayed her hips and turned her neck, just so, to catch the weak men's adoration in her small town of Las Nueces, Durango. Las Nueces was a sleepy little town where most people worked hard, but there was always a gem to be acquired, just like her.

Today, she wore a red bow in her hair and a pretty white lace dress, too fancy for common chores. From a distance, he thought he could smell her scent. He smiled as she flirted with a man carrying Coke bottles. He stumbled when she said hello, the poor man dropping half of his wares.

The stranger chuckled and slicked his own hair back. For good measure, he shined his shoes one more time. Tonight, he would introduce himself at the town dance, and he had no doubt that she would dance with him. And only him.

BY THE TIME SHE GOT HOME, her mother was nagging her.

"What took you so long? Your uncle will be here soon!"

Her mother wore a black skirt and dark buttoned blouse. She glanced at her daughter who dropped the bowl on the table.

She scowled. "What are you wearing?"

Rosa Maria smirked. "It is *so* hot, and this is the only thin dress I own."

"Take that off and put some decent clothes on!" said her mother as she chopped a carrot, almost nicking her index finger.

She did as commanded, only because she wanted to wear the dress later that night. She changed into a thin cotton housedress that clung to her body. Rosa Maria admired her long hair in the mirror and loved the flush of her cheeks. Her curves were the envy of most women, and she cherished her small waist. She would never have children and ruin her figure. That was for certain.

The banging in the kitchen mirrored her mother's stress, which pulled her out of her reverie. Rosa Maria regretted not having any lipstick because her mother said only whores wore lipstick. She longed for nail polish and mascara. She was about to curl her hair, when her mother bellowed her name. Last time her mother had gotten so angry at her, she had burned Rosa Maria's best dress because some nosy neighbor lady said she thought she had seen Rosa Maria at the dance, unchaperoned. She went back to the kitchen.

"Start mixing," her mother commanded.

Rosa Maria scoffed, but her mother was in no mood. The girl took what she thought was a decent amount of salt, a large handful, and mixed. She worried about her nails and winced at the next part. She grabbed a handful of the disgusting mess and was about to add lard, when her mother slapped her hand.

"Taste it."

Rosa Maria did. "It's too salty."

Her mother rolled her eyes and pulled out some cornmeal from the cupboard. It was just enough to make the tortillas acceptable. "We have to impress your uncle." Her mother frowned at the amount of lard.

Her mother said, "You don't need that. You're making tortillas, not tamales."

Rosa Maria scowled as she put half of the lard back in the container. Her greasy fingers repulsed her.

"Come on," her mother said.

"What's the point?" Rosa Maria asked and swayed her body. "I will marry a rich man and have maids. I'll never have to cook a day in my life."

Her mother laughed and watched as Rosa Maria struggled with a basic task. "If I ever die, you're going to starve."

Her mother added warm water and nodded approving of the job. "Go wash your hands and get some mint from the garden."

"I need to curl my hair!"

"Now."

Rosa Maria left in a huff.

Out in the small garden, she looked at the plants and had to smell them before she found the mint. She plucked what she thought was an acceptable amount, and then, she spotted him.

He wore a dark suit made of shiny material and beneath his fine jacket, a white silk shirt. Rosa Maria had never seen such a refined gentleman.

What could he be doing here? she wondered.

He rode a black horse and tipped his hat at her, giving her a warm smile. Rosa Maria licked her own lips as she stared at his perfect white teeth. His skin was sublime, even better than hers. She tried to pretend not to be interested, but she couldn't help but search his eyes.

This is the man I'm going to marry, she thought. In that instant, that was all it took to fall in love. He grew near her and was just a few feet away. He looked beyond to the horizon, and Rosa Maria was perplexed that he would not speak to her.

On impulse, she said, "How are you this fine morning?"

He rode away without saying a word to her. Men didn't usually ignore her. She stared at his back longer than she should have. Rosa Maria crushed the mint plants in her hand and went back to her mother.

Her mother took the leaves and put some in the stew.

She said, "Go sweep the floors."

Rosa Maria raised her hands and spat back, "I am not doing more work. The floor looks fine, and I have to go curl my hair!"

Rosa Maria left to her room. She had a brand-new curling iron that plugged into the wall. It had been a present from one of her admirers who owned the local furniture store and had been to the States in Mississippi. He had bought it for his wife and on a whim, gave it to her. The gift caused divisions in his marriage, but Rosa Maria hadn't promised him anything in return. She was sure it cost a fortune. It was better than the iron rods people used which often singed their hair.

Rosa Maria curled each ringlet. When she was done, she pinned the upper left and right corners like she had seen in the American movies. She put on a decent blue dress and went to the living room. She had spent a good forty minutes curling her hair, but her uncle was still not there.

Without thinking, she grabbed the broom and swept the small house. She sneezed at the cloud of dust and yelped as a small scorpion ran from under a chair. She killed it and did a better job of sweeping under the sofa and chairs. She swept the dirt out of the front door and put the broom away.

Her mother finished setting the table and kept staring out the window.

Riding the old mare her father had given him, Uncle Thomas arrived soon after. He was a brusque man and offered a gruff greeting. She went to him and gave him a kiss on the cheek. He reeked of cows. She noticed that he still wore his work clothes.

Rosa Maria smiled and had him sit at the head of the table.

Her mother served him, while they exchanged pleasantries. Her uncle was a man of few words. He mostly answered her mother's questions. After he was finished eating, her mother waited. Rosa Maria was certain she was asking for another loan. Since her father died a year ago, she struggled to make ends meet as a seamstress. And though Rosa Maria finished high school, she was not the brightest student. There was no work she could do and wanted to be taken care of as she deserved.

He looked at Rosa Maria and at her mother. "Well, it's settled."

Her mother clasped her hands. "Praise the Lord!"

"What is settled?" asked Rosa Maria.

Uncle Thomas gave her a side glance and explained, "Don Sebastian's oldest son saw you at the plaza a few Sundays ago. He wants to marry you."

Rosa Maria sat dumbfounded. Yes, she was eighteen years old and needed a steady suitor, but she had heard rumors of this eldest son. He was well to do, the son of a rancher a few towns over, but he had been burned in a fire. She also recalled he was an avid gambler and drinker. She had no idea what he looked like, and she would be damned if she married an ugly man with bad habits. She was about to object, but her mother gave her a stern look.

"He will come to meet you this Sunday, after church," he concluded and said his goodbyes. He was about to leave and added, "Look, I hear the rumors. Be on your best behavior when he visits, Rosa Maria."

"Oh, Uncle," she said, "I haven't even kissed a boy yet." Of course, that was not true. She had kissed plenty of men, but she hadn't been stupid enough to do more than that. Even when the mill's former owner tried to put his hands up her skirt in exchange for a few kilos of maize.

Her uncle went to leave as her mother gave him a sack full of gifts for his wife and three daughters. All goody two-shoes.

No doubt she's giving them each an ugly dress fit for a nun, Rosa Maria thought.

When her uncle left, she ranted about not wanting to marry the Sebastian boy. "I can have any boy I want! Why am I going to marry some rancher's son?"

Her mother slapped her and said, "I barely make enough for us to live on. You're a fool if you think anyone decent in the village is going to want to marry you! You think I don't hear the stories? What were you doing last week with that idiot who runs the local shop?"

Rosa Maria rubbed her cheek and was about to get another one, when her mother said, "And don't even think about going to the dance tonight!"

It was Friday night, and her village held a dance every month. Rosa Maria often snuck out and managed to make it back before midnight but made sure a couple of her trusted friends walked her home. After all, it was one thing to kiss boys and quite another to have real rumors of her being a slut—which she wasn't. Not really.

IT WAS 9:00 P.M. AND LIKE CLOCKWORK, her mother fell asleep at the chair doing some extra sewing. Rosa Maria touched up her hair a bit and put on her lace dress. She wore simple silk flats her father bought in Texas. One last gift for his princess. Of course, she wanted high heels.

She had no red lipstick but managed to put on some white powder. She looked virginal, her upturned nose delicate. Her face was Hollywood perfect. Light-skinned and the envy of most girls. She admired her full lips, but wished her eyes were blue. They were honey brown.

Rosa Maria took a black shawl and snuck out of the house. She sped to the town hall, and outside was her best friend, Tila.

"Just look at you!" Tila was nineteen years old. Tonight, she wore an orange dress that covered most of her curves and showed no cleavage. She also had a crush on Mr. Sanchez, the mill owner. But he married Tila's cousin a couple of months ago. No one could tell if he was happy or not.

When they entered, the hall was already full of people dancing a fast-paced dance. She went with Tila to grab a drink. Heads turned towards them. A young man just turned seventeen was going to ask her to dance, but she averted him, putting Tila between them. They grabbed their drinks and sat at the table. Rosa Maria gave her a glum look.

"What is it?" asked Tila over the din of the music.

The song changed to a slow waltz, so they lowered their voices. Three people asked her out to dance, but she declined saying her stomach hurt. Rosa Maria explained her predicament, and her friend squealed with delight.

"A son of Don Sebastian!"

Rosa Maria shushed her as a few girls turned to look at them. "Be quiet!" She leaned in close.

"I heard his face is badly burned," Rosa Maria continued.

Tila shook her head. "Nonsense—"

The music stopped as he walked into the hall. He was wearing the same clothes as before, but Rosa Maria's heart stopped along with every girl of marriageable age and even some married ones. Tila also held her breath, then exhaled. "Who is that?"

The stranger held her gaze and walked towards her table, as people parted the way. He extended a hand without even asking.

It was a magical moment. She breathed in his scent as another melancholy waltz began. It was Pedro Infante's "The

Nights of October", a song Rosa Maria wanted played as her wedding song.

She looked into his eyes as he spun her around. Rosa Maria thought they were made for each other. He had light skin and dark curls. What struck her the most were his blue eyes. Every time he smiled at her, she wanted to swoon, but she was too strong for that.

"What's your name?" she finally asked.

"Nicholas," he answered and added no other details. Other men glared at the stranger, but none dared, cut in. They danced for over an hour, but Rosa Maria was so enveloped in him she did not notice the passing of time. Round and round they went without taking a break. She was delighted at his grace. He never missed a step and knew how to dance the twist on down to a ranchera without sweating all over her. He was a man of few words, but she didn't care as long as *she* was his universe.

Near midnight he asked, "Do you want to go for a ride?"

The question, of course, was complex. Leaving with him would cause the town to buzz with rumors of a love affair, and she wasn't sure if he would steal her away to some remote location and deflower her. Rosa Maria thought about her uncle and her mother. She scrutinized his left hand. He had no wedding band, but on his pinky was a gorgeous gold ring with a large emerald.

"Are you married?" she asked point blank.

Without skipping a beat, he answered, "No."

Rosa Maria calculated. He could be lying of course, but he did not seem to be conniving. Nicholas was suave and graceful, but he wasn't a liar. She could tell when someone was lying to her, as she was an avid conniver, when she needed to be.

She looked towards Tila who gave her a worried look as she walked to get her shawl.

"Don't," Tila said grabbing Rosa Maria's arm, but she shook her off and went with him anyway.

Nicholas was an absolute gentleman. He sat her on the back of the horse behind him, as a lady should ride. She had ridden like that many times before with her father, and she was not afraid of horses. They rode past the mill towards the river.

"Where are we going?" she asked but got no answer.

The horse began to pick up speed. The wind was blowing through her hair, and she found it exhilarating. He curved past the river and sped away down a rocky path. She had to grip his back, and almost fell off. He took a sharp turn, and she lost her shawl. The horse rode faster than any beast should. She turned back. The town was ever-so far away for the minutes they had been together. Nicholas next raced up to a strange place filled with thorns and brambles.

The horse was just as nimble when raced.

She cried, "Can you please stop?"

The horse sprinted up a steep mountain Rosa Maria had never been to before. The horse sped up an impossible vertical incline. She clung for dear life, as they entered a large cave. It was pitch dark.

Rosa Maria was relieved when the horse slowed. Through the darkness, the horse continued down a series of tunnels descending downwards. They stopped at a level place. Nicholas dismounted and grabbed her and threw her down on the ground. The fall knocked the wind out of her, but she fought striking at emptiness.

He gripped her wrists and tied them painfully. He lifted her up. Her feet trailed, dancing above the ground. She was suspended high, unable to wrest free.

SHE STRUGGLED until she fell asleep from exhaustion. He traced his fingers down the curve of her neck. In her sleep, she gave a small cry. Nicholas turned her back towards him and began.

First, his nails extended themselves into flawless instruments, one inch each. He stroked her back, all the way down to her perfect waist. He raked his nails down her back enjoying every second.

THE BURNING PAIN in her back awoke her. She screamed as he raked his fingers down her back again, from the nape of her neck to her buttocks. He spun her around and kissed her. Rosa Maria felt like coal entered her mouth. The pain was excruciating—radiating through her whole mouth—outside and inside.

Even as she was tortured, she was worried that her mouth would be permanently scarred and that the blood would stain her shoes. She wondered if her mother could sew the dress back or cut the back out, somehow.

As if he was reading her mind he said, "I can offer more than rags."

She whispered, "I don't want anything from you, you piece of filth."

He smirked and was about to kiss her face, but he stopped. "I'm not touching your pretty face. I'm not supposed to leave any area unscathed, but your face is so lovely."

Bile rose from her throat, and the pain grew worse. He took a dirty finger and ran it around her lips soothing them. Then, he stuck his thumb in her mouth. No man had ever done that to her. It was sensuous, but repulsive. She wanted to gag, and at the same time moan in contentment. The pain lessened.

Five surrounding torches lit all at once. She spat at him and when the spittle landed on his face, it sizzled.

"Who are you?" she cried, but deep down, she knew who he was.

WHO WAS HE? The truth is he didn't know anymore. Centuries ago, he had been a devoted father, but smallpox killed his wife and five children. He had been tempted, as he was tempting Rosa Maria now, but he chose poorly.

She was strong. Perhaps stronger than he had been, even though she was young. He smiled at her. She cringed. He kissed her again, this time doing so gently without heat. She bit his tongue, drawing blood, and his laughter echoed through the cave.

He brought a tin of water, and she drank against her better judgement. She wanted to spit it in his face but was parched. He caressed her cheek and was pleased to see she did not flinch.

"I do care about you," he said.

He unhooked her and lay her down on the dirt. She fell asleep in due time, and he went to get some dry jerky. He turned his back and reached for his satchel. A sharp pain on the back of his head made him yelp as Rosa Maria kicked him and ran down a dark passage.

"Clever girl," he said rubbing the injury. He marveled that she outwitted him, if for a short spell.

He walked listening. He couldn't let her get far, or she might be killed. He found her a few minutes later, crawling on her hands and knees. Nicholas picked her up and threw her over his shoulder.

She fought and scratched and pulled his hair. He tied her hands and feet and placed her in the exact spot.

She screamed, and he jammed the jerky in her mouth. She wanted to curse, but instead chewed. Rosa Maria was plotting, he was certain. He bent over and kissed her forehead which raised a tirade of insults.

She fell asleep after a time, as he watched over her, making sure nothing disturbed her peace.

WHEN SHE WOKE, she was hanging on the hook again. This time, he scratched her arms and legs, being careful not to touch her face. He looked pained every time he clawed her. The agony was unbearable, but her rage was stronger.

Suddenly, he stopped, and like magic, he soothed every wound. He worried she would scar.

Why did he care so much? he asked himself.

Thirteen hours had passed, and she was still awake. She glared at him and tried to spit, but her mouth was dry.

He flinched, when she sneered at him. At first, he couldn't understand what she said. He grew closer.

"So, you weren't man enough to get a woman, so you have to steal stupid girls away." She kicked and impacted his penis. He bent over as she laughed for the first time in a long time since her father died.

"Wretched girl!" he howled, and she fainted in terror. The transformation had been a reflex. First, his eyes went back from a glowing amber to a sky blue. His fangs receded, but his pointed ears were slow to become human.

It took thirty minutes for him to go back to normal. He caressed the curve of her neck. She was beautiful. She woke with a start and began to fight.

He sat there watching her until she calmed down. Normally, he would wait another day, but her stubbornness was unlike any he had seen in centuries.

Out of nowhere, two tables appeared. One of them was laden with jewelry and a rich red dress, like the one she wanted. At the center was a set of high heels. They were a fantasy come true.

To the right were ordinary rags. A metal basin with a washboard and a coarse apron.

"You can have a life of luxury," he said pointing to the table with elegant articles. "You can stay young forever. Have any man you want."

He saw the light in her eyes as she stared at the shoes. He knew she would love them but realized the adoration in her eyes ran deep.

"Or." He paused gesturing towards the other table. "You can have a life of drudgery. You will marry a simple man, but never be rich. Ever."

THE SHOES SHIMMERED in the fire light. They were exquisitely curved and the heels the perfect height. The dress was the material of dreams. She stared at the alluring table, and her eyes rested on the drab table.

"Well," he said, "as soon as you make your choice. This ends."

She would not choose. Most people would have been screaming one way or the other, but she was weighing her options.

He smiled. "If you choose this life," he continued pointing at the life of boredom, "you will always have to be obedient, always do good."

"Or what?" she asked.

"Or this will seem like child's play." He ran his fingers against a wall making a grating noise.

"If you choose the other life," he said, "you will never want or suffer. You will never grow old."

There was no way she could be obedient forever, and she dreaded the thought of growing old like her neighbor. She looked down. By now, her dress was rags, and she hung, naked, but he never touched her. Not there.

Rosa Maria thought long about what she wanted. She screamed as a burning pain ran up her left thigh. It was his hands that were burning her. He was no magician. In fact, she had figured out who he was. He ran his hand down her right thigh. That same look of pain on his face made her shout.

"You don't want to do this! Stop."

He hesitated but spun her around and proceeded to burn her back. He traced his fingers all around her.

This went on for what seemed like an eternity, but then, she thought about her father and how much he loved her. She thought about how much her mother struggled. No one would want her now, but the promise of youth. That made her pause.

"Stop!" she said, "Stop, devil."

She looked at him, as a small smile curved his lips. He grabbed her by the hips, this time without burning her. He grew close to her face, so he could hear, and breathed in her scent of sweat and pain, as she whispered into his ear.

HE LEFT HER in the middle of the desert. It was Sunday morning, and he knew they were near. Soon, he spied them, a group of five men. Her choice had surprised him, no doubt, but he was glad of it.

He saw as a young man on a chestnut horse picked her up gently. They rode away, and Nicholas gave her one last longing look. He would never see Rosa Maria again.

THE NEXT DAY, she walked in the plaza arm in arm with Armando Sebastian. Two months had gone by, and she was still wearing long-sleeved clothes and a long skirt to cover her scratches and burns.

She looked at his straight brown hair. He would steal a mischievous glance and smile. Nicholas had lied to her; he was not a plain man. There were burn marks on his neck that his collar could not hide, but that didn't matter to her anymore.

He sat on the bench with her and asked her if she wanted something from the vendor. She shook her head. The last few weeks she had slimmed down. The doctor said she was dehydrated and had suffered a shock. The day she was returned, her mother brought the priest, but all she said to him was that she had been punished.

Now, as she sat by her suitor, she admired his strong hands.

"They weren't always like that," he said.

She waited.

"I used to be a gambler and alcoholic," he said. "I don't remember everything that happened, like you can't remember everything. I still have nightmares. I guess you don't completely forget. For me, it was a gorgeous woman named Isabella. She offered me a career in the States away from all of this boredom, but. . . ." He pointed at his back.

Her mouth dropped.

"I made the right choice, as you did," he said. "You know what saved me?"

She shook her head.

"The image of my mother crying over my absence. I couldn't break her heart."

Rosa Maria breathed in and confessed, "For me it was my father. He loved me so much. I also thought about my mother who works so hard. I think he, Nicholas, promised me youth and riches, but I don't recall exactly. Just that the temptation was awesome."

He laughed. "Ah, yes. Well, I can't give you youth." He kissed her hand, and she blushed.

He added. "You will never want for anything."

She laughed, which perplexed him. "He lied to me." Rosa Maria looked down and appreciated how shined and clean his boots were.

"I'm a terrible cook," she admitted.

"Your mother told me," he said and smiled. "I have my flaws. I can't stand disorder, and I struggle with anger."

She flinched.

"I won't ever hurt you," he stammered. "It's just my cross to bear."

She turned to him and asked, "Why me?"

"You are very pretty, to be sure," he said, "but that is not why I noticed you."

Armando explained that when he saw her in the plaza, she had given the local beggar her last change. It wasn't the first time he had seen her. That was the third time. Another time, he spied her giving nuts to a little girl and another saw her give a mangy dog some tortillas. Armando saw what few people rarely saw in her, kindness and compassion.

"Besides," he said, "I have no room to judge. I took me a while to figure out how to plant corn. Horses, no problem, but when it came to actual hard work, I was a joke. You will figure it out, and my mother and sisters will help you. I will as well."

A life of drudgery, she thought.

"Besides, I was thinking our village needed a new dress shop. Your mother could help you," he said. "I've seen her handiwork." He pointed to his elaborate shirt.

Nicholas had been lying as had all the town gossips. Armando was offering her a dream she had never thought of and her mother a means to live.

In the end, she accepted not for the wealth he offered. She accepted because he shared her pain and was more than she could imagine in a husband. He saw the best in her and didn't judge her. Since she had returned, most of the men in the village said she had been raped and that she deserved it. A lot of women agreed.

For the rest of her life, she would always wonder what life would have been like had she chosen youth and riches, but deep down, she knew she made the right choice.

Unforgiveable

He spied her in the mirror's reflection. She had gorgeous golden hair and morose silver eyes. Her face had what the gueros called a sweet heart shape, though a bit elongated, with a perfect nose and kissable lips. Her eyes are what had attracted him the most; he imagined that those eyes never judged anyone, like when he struck out at the semi-finals. Her skin was flawless, and he swore, glowed. She was slender like an alfalfa stalk, not voluptuous like her cheerleader friends, and when she smiled his heart would melt. If her father could see him spying from the window, he would shoot him on the spot and be justified for it. That Tuesday was the 40th time he had come to visit her.

He peeked over the expansive ranch-style window, with imprisoning bars, but she was so absorbed with her primping and beautifying that her eyes fixated on her reflection. It was a hot July summer day, in Silver, Arizona, and despite the heat, she looked fresh. *How did she manage to keep her hair so bouncy, even outdoors, when he was sweating like a pig?* She pinched a make-up brush between her delicate fingers and fluttered it over her cheeks. One at a time.

"Girl, you're perfect. You don't need all of that on your face," he whispered to her, tracing a circle around his own face.

This was it. This was the moment. He held his breath and was about to rap on her window, but an acidic hiss startled him out of his renewed courage. There was that black mangy cat, Nightling that she loved so much. It hissed again with its hair standing on end and took a swipe at him.

"Mind your own business, fool!" He hissed back.

He peeked one more time through the window, as she looked up, but he ducked before she saw him. Beto crept back towards the desert. The dilapidated trailer he called home was over the wall, a five-minute walk away. As he inched home, he felt the hot breath of Mr. Stan's hideous Rottweiler on his backside. It snarled sending spittle at his face. Beto screamed and ran. With Beto's every step, the ugly beast drew closer, lunging and snapping its teeth on the empty wind behind him. At last, he leaped over the adobe wall that surrounded her property. Only then, as his heart raced, did he realize how loud the dog was barking. He would have to keep running unless he be discovered still.

The dog stopped and spun around when Sarah's dulcet cries called it back. He wished with all of his heart she would someday call out to him like that. As he beat that near-death experience, he imagined her cheering for him in her short uniform, her hair bouncing up and down, a red pompom erect in her left hand. As she jumped, she spelled out his nickname, not his full name, *B. E. T. O.*—the crowd cheering. He gave her his best smile, as he caught glances of her white underwear, and tipped his cap towards her. He was the best runner, after all, and that leap over the wall had been better than any video game parkour. He took off his baseball jersey and mopped his brow. *A. Andrades* it read in embroidered black letters. He took a deep breath stilling the internal pummeling in his chest, put it back on, and left.

He walked, kicking at desert lizards every now and then and sang a sad song about a woman who lost her husband on Christmas Eve. The wife wandering eternally for a love she would never reunite with—like he and Sarah.

"Life is so unfair," he told a gliding hawk that landed near him. It was majestic, a rich brown, surely one with a faithful mate. Beto continued singing as loud as he could, as the dust storm began to darken the air around him. He sang louder—now that no one could see or hear him—sucking in dust.

He would have given up all the songs he knew to be with her, even just for one night. He blinked against the irritating sheet of sand. It wasn't impossible to see through it, but the eerie haze put his senses on alert. He turned back and swore someone walked behind him, but all he saw was the light brown wall. Minutes later, he reached the lonely patch of desert and entered the run-down trailer that was more an oven than home. The small swamp cooler in the living room had died, and he had none of his father's penchant for mechanics.

"It's a dust-filled purgatory. Out there *and* in here," he muttered, as he grew drowsy from the heat. He sat on an old plastic chair and stared at the far wall.

Nearly four weeks ago, Beto's father and mother had not returned after a long day of work, and he was certain they had been deported. His father was a mechanic at Desert Mobile, which Beto thought was a stupid name. His mother loved her job at the oldest Jack in the Box in the city. He called it Jack in the Crack, which his friends thought was a stupid name. He still went looking for her every day. But now he didn't bother to ask her colleagues. When he first inquired, they had all been bashful, in the way undocumented workers can be.

He just sat and waited, an orphan customer without money.

Weeks before, when he went to the shop where his father had worked, all the men were cursing over their cars and paid him no attention.

The one good person who said anything was an elderly blind man sitting on a metal bench. "Ain't seen your dad since last week. D'you call the police?"

Beto was too afraid to call the police. *What if they took him away and put him in a foster home with a pervert or worse— deported him?* He didn't know anyone in Mexico, and his relatives constantly mocked his Spanish. Instead, Beto had given the kind man his cell number. He punched the number with nimble fingers, but Beto's crappy cell phone had also run out of monthly minutes. Still, he managed to keep up appearances and was lucky school had been out before his parents vanished.

He made the food in fridge and cupboard last as long as possible. But sometimes, he would steal eggs from his neighbors' chicken coops. On Wednesday he killed a jackrabbit with his dad's gun. He knew it was a matter of time before he would have to tell the counselor or somebody that he needed help, but that wouldn't be until August. He was just so terrified of ending up like his cousins whose parents had been deported last year. They went into foster care, taken in by a drunk ex-marine who hurt them on a regular basis. Angela was four and Diego was the same age as him, 17. Seventeen and unable to protect his sister.

If Beto had a car or his dad's old truck, he would have gotten a job, but the places he walked to, ignored his queries and applications.

He tensed, the weight of his woes heavy on his shoulders and looked at the can of tuna, so small in the dark cabinet. He hated tuna. But he loved fried food, so in the end, he made flour empanadas, small turnovers, just like his mom taught him. He kneaded the flour in the rhythmic way his mother, his ever-patient saint, showed him. Afterward, he added a little bit of water and lard. He rolled out each flat circle, missing his mother more with each one he finished. By evening, he was done with the half moons—six total. He fried each one with as little lard as possible, but they still browned to his satisfaction, not quite a deep fry, but a light yellow one.

His heart sank when he realized most of the lard was gone. When he was done, he stared at his soggy, meager meal. He must have done something wrong, he figured, as he held one up with his hands. It flopped.

"Idiot." He had forgotten to squeeze out the water from the tuna. It was then, he made a difficult decision. He knew it wasn't right, but he had no money and couldn't ask for help. He would have to break into houses, and soon.

BETO KNEW WHERE HE WOULD START. The guy three trailers down was a meth head. There was no doubt about it as people came and went at all hours of the night, sometimes even kids on cool shiny bikes. It wouldn't have been out of order to see kids on bikes fit for sandy trails, but they would come at 1:00 a.m., 2:00 a.m., 3:00 a.m., with no parents in sight. There was one night Leo Hark would not be in his trailer; every third Saturday of the month.

That Saturday he would go across the border to Tito's Tango, another stupid name, but a great place to party. Beto had been there himself a couple of times. In fact, that is where he had first seen Sarah grinding against some idiot football player. She had been wearing tight jeans and a simple white tank top, but Beto swore she had an aura around her whole being. He stared at her until his friends started egging him on to ask her out. Of course, he hadn't.

Leo Hark had as much luck with the ladies as Beto and was always looking for love in all the wrong places. That night he was glad of Leo's miserable love life. Beto didn't bother with any ceremony. He walked over to Hark's trailer and made sure it was dark. He could see every detail through the moonlight. No one was home. He took a large brick and broke the window closest to a dumpy, red sofa. Using a wooden crate, Beto got in careful not to cut himself.

He listened for any dogs, but there were none. The trailer was near-empty with the sad sofa in the living room. He rummaged through the cupboards. All Leo had were chicken Ramen packets and a can of turnips. Beto felt the weight of the turnips and for a moment thought about throwing the can against the wall. Still, it was better than nothing. When he opened the fridge, his heart sank. It was empty, except for some bottles and assorted chemicals. The freezer was equally dismal with a big block of weed. He had hoped to find steak or some hidden money in ice cube trays like a bad B-movie.

"Who puts weed in the freezer?" He frowned and considered the weed, but he thought about his team. There was no way he was getting kicked off the team. It was one thing to break into a junkie's trailer. But selling was a real crime.

From the dark hall, he heard wheezing. Beto turned, afraid he would see the end of a gun. In the darkness, emerged a sick old man, skeletal and gaunt. His mouth drooled like a pendejo[1], but his eyes were furious.

The old man shouted, "Get out!"

The voice was so loud, it filled the room and the cavernous part of Beto's chest. He didn't have to be told twice. Beto ran out of there and lost all of the Ramen, as he scrambled out the window.

He fled for his life and turned back to hear the old man scream an ethereal scream that made all the hairs on his arms

---

[1] Someone stupid

stand up. He ran for over ten minutes, frightening nocturnal animals, including a family of three small white owls. Just to be safe, he took a circuitous route around a nearby citrus orchard.

He reached the trailer and was glad to see his old pal Chuckey sitting on the front steps. Chuckey was an old Chihuahua, going on eight years, and for once, he was grateful his dog was an unconscionable puto[2] who went to all the barrio houses hooking up with his doggie girlfriends. Someone was feeding it well; its body was growing pudgy, its face full.

"Did you bring me any?"

His little brown dog smiled shameless and barked its high-pitched bark. Beto opened the door.

"Come on, walk in." Chuckey sat without budging, so he picked up his friend and went back to bed.

"Shit," he said to Chuckey, "if I can get to church, I can use the pantry. Why didn't I think of that?"

Chuckey barked until Beto tucked it in bed, but his companion kept yipping aggravated at phantoms. Beto looked out the window, and his heart froze. There was a dark figure there. The face was difficult to discern, even with the full moon. The man was tall, and what troubled Beto is that he couldn't make out the stranger's eyes.

He thought, *Had the old man followed him?* There was no way that skinny old man had kept up. After all, Beto was one of the best players on his J.V. baseball team and could sprint faster than any baseball player in any high school. Besides, the sick old man had been leaning over and could barely walk.

The man was at least six feet tall, standing at a distance, nine yards away. There was something menacing about him. As if mirroring his fear, Chuckey began to howl a deep mournful howl of

---

[2] A male whore

death. Beto locked the doors and made sure the windows were secure. The man just stood there staring at the trailer.

"Fuck it." Beto grabbed a metal bat from his small closet and went to confront the man.

He shouted, "What do you want puto?"

But he was gone. He scanned the horizon in every direction. Beto searched around the trailer, even under the trailer. There was no one around.

He asked confused, "What?"

Chuckey came out with its tail between its legs. Picking the chunky mass up, Beto soothed it, but Chuckey wouldn't be calmed. It whined. Beto put it down, and it ran off in the opposite direction of where the man had been. Perhaps, to meet one of its bitches.

"Some friend you are," muttered Beto.

The trailer seemed emptier than before, and he wished he had a gaming station to waste time. The shadows in the small living room grew darker. Like a sissy eight-year-old, Beto turned on the lights and checked the trailer. No one was there. He looked out the window towards Sarah's expansive ranch house, which he could see at a distance, and his heart stopped for a second time. The man was standing outside her property facing towards her window as Beto had so many times before.

"The hell?" he said to no one and grabbed his bat. He ran towards the stranger; this time without a shred of fear in his soul.

Beto loved to run on any occasion. His father dubbed him El Barrio Road Runner. He was faster than any of his teammates, and if he had a better batting average, he would have made the varsity team. He was sure of it. Within minutes, he reached her place, but again, the man vanished. Beto decided to check if she was okay. He knew he was risking getting shot at by her crazy father, but he had to be sure. He snuck in and was glad her ugly dog was not patrolling and ready to bite his butt.

She was asleep with her back turned towards him. He waited a while as he watched her breath rise and fall. Without warning, her father turned on the kitchen lights, which he could see below her room door. He was forever shouting.

Man, thought Beto, *the man is always on the same loop.*

He raged about everything from his coffee being weak to his shirt having a stain. At one point, he vented against the poor dog. Just as the list of grievances started, the man stopped.

"Come with me," said a soft voice from behind.

Beto turned, swung, with perfect form, and hit air with his bat, then slammed the brick wall with full force. He yelped; the nerves from his fingers sent painful signals up his arm as the bat twanged against the wall. He shook his hands fast, hoping to ease the pain. He turned around, but the man was not there. The adrenaline rushed through his body as he tensed.

He thought, *Where did he go?*

He heard the voice again, everywhere and nowhere. *Come with me.*

He lost his courage, but, somehow, managed to check the property. He circled back to her bedroom window and was going to check the garage, until her father slammed open the front door.

"YOU SEE! IT IS ALL YOUR FAULT!" her father bellowed, "YOUR FAULT! YOU SLUT!"

Beto didn't wait a moment. He ran faster than when his team, The Scorpions, played versus The Chiefs (another stupid name) and tied 7 to 7. He hit a fastball with that same perfect form and ran like the devil was after him. When he slid home, he had botched the slide losing his right shoe, but no one noticed. He reached home base as he scraped his right foot on pebbles and sand. The crowd had cheered as he won the game. Even The Chiefs had patted him on the back.

Luck was on his side. Her father hadn't seen him, or the crazy fool would have shot him and been justified.

"Dude must need glasses. I was right there."

He jogged back, making sure the front and back doors were locked again. He waited, his ears tuned to the softest cricket song. He stood for fifteen minutes before he moved. Beto went into his father's room and took out the nine-millimeter that his dad kept under the bed. The gun was heavy, cold, a death machine he despised. Like most Mexican parents, his papa had shown him how to shoot since Beto was seven. He loaded the gun and pulled the clip. Snap! The sound filled the hollow trailer, making the stillness more awful, and Beto almost started crying.

His mother made the small trailer cozy with small desert potted plants here and there and beautiful wall pictures. Some of which she embroidered herself with yarn from the discount table. They showed scenes from her pueblito, Rio Fresco, another stupid name, and a place he had never visited because he didn't have papers. She was so attentive to detail, he wondered with dread why she hadn't called his school, even from Mexico. She had the office phone memorized and could make herself understood in her broken English.

He mimicked her, "Hello? This Beto's Mom? Please, eh, tell Beto, eh, he is en mucho poo poo. Si."

He chuckled, put the safety on his companion, and nestled the gun under the far-right pillow with the barrel pointing towards the wall. He decided to call the gun Anti-Puto and dared the man to show his face near his place again.

He was ready for the dark man.

WHOEVER HE WAS, he didn't show up the next day, but Beto scanned the horizon on the hour. By 6:00 p.m., he was convinced the Dark Puto, as he dubbed the stranger, was not coming back, so he went to visit his girl.

First, Beto searched for her father's monstrous red truck. It was gone, and he knew her father wouldn't return until later that evening. He listened. He grabbed a rock and threw it over the fence hitting a potted plant. It made a loud enough sound that would draw that black nightmare out. Beto peeked over the wall again and jumped over it with more grace than the previous night.

He ducked as he neared her window. There she was again, this time ironing her uniform. Beto loved how methodical she was in everything she did. He noticed she was wearing nothing but her underwear. He paused and would have kept staring, but he wasn't a pervert. He hid under the wall until he was sure she was done ironing.

When he looked over again, she was wearing her purple pajamas that were juvenile for someone so gorgeous. She adjusted the waistband and stared at herself in the mirror.

"Girl," he said, "you're not fat at all. Stop staring at your perfect navel."

In the distance, he heard the familiar engine roar, and that was all he needed to hear as he ran back over the wall.

THE NEXT DAY, HE JOGGED TO THE SCHOOL and was devastated by what he heard. It was a ridiculous enterprise, to do so in the heat, but he had gone at 7:00 a.m. to meet them like he did every Wednesday at 9:00 a.m., once school was out. His boys used to always hang out on the bleachers and drink out of sports bottles. So, he ran like an idiot for 45 minutes before he got there. He waited, but he must have taken longer than he thought because when he arrived, they were already there, sitting and drinking from Carlos' signature orange bottle. He was startled when he saw Jeff Carranza crying. They hadn't seen him, so he snuck up behind them planning a spectacular prank.

He was about to pull down Jeff's pants, when he heard Jeff say, "That idiot Beto! Stupid, stupid Beto!"

"Coach is never going to be able to replace him," said his best friend Carlos. He was the same height as he, charming with a constant gaggle of cheerleaders that gravitated towards him. Cool confident Carlos. Beto knew the girls loved him for his near-blonde curls and green eyes. Plus, Carlos was born in the U.S., while his dark brown self, though quite handsome, was just a wetback. He eavesdropped as someone else ranted about how stupid he had been.

What the hell were they talking about? Was he kicked off the team? For what?

Jeff sobbed, taking a huge swallow. His fiery red hair was matted against is dead-colored skin with peppered freckles.

Jeff said, "Why'd he have to go drinking like that? That was so *stupid*." In a fit, he grabbed the bottle, threw it, and smashed it almost hitting the pitching mound.

They protested in unison, as Jeff heaved inconsolably. Carlos pulled out another bottle from somewhere.

"Come on," said Peter McFarland, the only team member Beto hated. He smiled with his white teeth, his trendy haircut highlighting his Anglo features, long bangs reaching blue eyes.

Peter spat, "We don't need that spic. We never needed him." Everyone stopped.

"What did you say?" asked Carlos tensing up like a backyard rooster about to strike. "You take that back, you racist asshole!"

Peter stood up, inches from Carlos. Peter was four inches shorter, but far more arrogant.

"Come on now guys," said someone. "You know how Coach feels about fighting! You two better stop it!"

Carlos swung first, making contact with Peter's nose. Peter didn't even blink, and Beto stared fascinated as a couple of tears streamed down that smug face. Beto was sure his nose was broken, and still, that jerk kneed Carlos in the groin, which brought the team to tear them apart. Despite the pain, to his credit, Carlos still lunged at Peter, who sneered his typical sneer as blood ran down his perfect face. Before anyone could notice, Beto ran back home.

WHEN HE REACHED THE TRAILER, he was bawling. The sand caked on his face and inside his throat. He didn't care. Beto knew real men didn't cry, but there was so much he could take.

He thought, *Damnit! Why were they talking about him like that? That piece of garbage Peter McFarland had a special place in hell reserved for him, that dirty fighting puto.*

And what was up with Jeff? Jeff was hard, always playing at being so tough, despite his goofy clown hair.

Damn! He wished he had a phone. *That was it.*

He was going to break into a house and call Carlos. Besides, a dreadful thought had emerged as he reached his trailer.

Carlos couldn't fight worth a damn. Beto was always the one fighting for his best friend because if Carlos got into any kind of trouble his Seventh Day Adventist mom would pull him off the team before he could say, "Praise Jehovah!"

He wondered, *What if he broke his fingers in a typical boxer injury? Stupid Carlos. He was the stupid one!*

He sat on the stairs and looked up outside his trailer, hoping to see Chuckey. Someone was staring at him.

There he was again. The man. Beto glared and realized he was unarmed. No trusty bat. No Anti-Puto.

"Screw it," he mumbled and marched forward. "What do you want?"

He neared at a steady pace. The man stood unmoving. As he got closer, he realized the man had thin features with near-white skin. Día de Muertos white.

He smiled, a kind smile, which infuriated Beto further. "I SAID WHAT DO YOU WANT?"

"Come with me. It's time," he said.

"What?" He screamed his chest heaving. "I ain't going nowhere with you!"

The man let out a slow breath and gave him a pleading look. "Your parents are waiting."

He looked uncertain at the lean face and paused. Just then he heard a scream. *Was that his girl?* He turned towards her voice, and when he confronted the man again, he was gone.

"What the hell is going on?" He looked at the sand where the man stood and stopped. The sand had been wiped clean by the wind.

He heard the scream which was louder than the first time and ran towards her house. Her violent father was raging, at who he wasn't certain. Beto didn't care. He was going to hurt her. He was sure of it. He barged in through the front door not caring about the consequences, but when he got there, the house was empty.

For the first time, he wondered if anything was real. "Am I dreaming?" He felt the warmth of the air as dusty particles danced before his eyes. Cocking his head to the side, he listened for them. A hiss brought him out his stupor.

"Shut up, you stupid cat!"

Nightling growled, annoying Beto beyond his limits. He left, but not before he checked her room. It was empty, peaceful. He inspected her bureau. There it was, a picture of Carlos and one of her cheerleading photos right next to it. She had made the illusion that they were standing close to each other, his picture taller than hers. He got closer and his heart ran to his throat. It wasn't Carlos at all.

It was *his* team picture. *Was that her red kiss on his chest?*

He looked around the room and paused. Resting on her chair was his letterman jacket, with blank sleeves, waiting for the coveted varsity letters. The one he had swept and mopped floors for months to purchase at his dad's shop. He had mowed his coach's lawn 10 times to get enough money.

"What?"

Nightling came again shrieking territorial noises, except, it brought two other cats. His head began to spin, from hunger and all the running in the heat. He would have fainted, if another mangy orange cat hadn't launched itself at Beto's face. He swatted it away at the last moment, but he wasn't about to mess with three crazy cats. He ran out of there taking one final look at the picture on her bureau. *Why were his things there, in her room?*

"What's going on?" He slowed and rested for a time before he started again. He wasn't sure where he was going, but he felt better and picked up the pace. The wind felt glorious against him. Beto got that familiar rush—that running high he loved so much. He ran down Avenue G towards Nopales, AZ. And a third of the way slowed down as he spied an altar. It was beautiful with fresh flowers in painted tin cans and a cross made of yellow plastic flowers. There were no pictures, just a date of when some poor shmuck had died. Something about it was familiar, but he couldn't recall what alcoholic had died there. It took a few minutes for him to remember why the image tugged at him so. His mother loved yellow roses. He stopped and said a quick Hail Mary, even though he didn't believe and kept running.

He wasn't tired, despite how dizzy he had been, and despite the heat that pounded down on every poor soul. He ran for another thirty minutes before he stopped at St. Mary's food pantry.

He walked in and said, -Buenas tardes.-[3]

The old woman heard the bell as he entered and said automatically, "One bag per person, including children." She had her back turned as she watched the early telenovela.

Beto smelled the fresh fruit and took in the abundance of food. The door slammed as a mother with a black eye and her child walked in. The daughter was a cute little girl with light brown hair and freckles all over her face.

She giggled at him and said, "Hi," and he waved back.

"One bag per person," said the lazy old woman without looking away from the counter.

Afterwards, fat Deacon Torrez walked in. He said, "Welcome. We have fresh bananas and some coconuts." He was wearing a loose green guayabera with denim shorts and black flip flops. He was almost the same height as Beto, which made the man tall by Mexican standards.

Beto smiled. "Hi Deacon."

Deacon Torrez gave the woman a broad smile and stooped down to greet the little girl, but he grew somber when he saw the mother's face. Before Beto could ask for help, the deacon went to the woman to talk about her predicament. She tugged at her long

---

[3] Good afternoon.

sleeves, as she covered numerous angry marks, and looked down. Before long, she went to his office to talk in private. Beto needed help, but he forgot about the deacon ignoring him, and grabbed everything he could cook. There were plenty of rows of tomato sauce and soup. He grabbed some chicken bouillon. Within minutes, the bag was full to the brim. Immediately after filling it, he dreaded the idea of carrying everything home, but he was so hungry, he didn't care.

The girl came up to him. "What's your name?"

"My name's Beto." He ruffled her hair, pleased to be talking to someone after so long.

"Your hands are cold," she said and stepped back.

"Your head is SO hot, shrimp." She smiled uncertain.

"Cindy, come here!" barked her mother.

What was it with white people yelling all the damned time?

He went about his business and neared the counter. He waited and waited.

He asked the woman, "Do I have to do anything else?"

The old woman looked over, sniffed, and went back to watching her T.V.

"Okay," he said with extra snark, "thank you for your service and dedication to the community, mam."

He turned hoping to talk to the deacon, but the woman's plight must have been pressing because he never returned.

"Why are men such pigs?" he asked out loud. He turned back trying to catch the old woman's attention, but she ignored him.

Then, he saw it. There it was like a dinosaur in Time Square—a black rotary phone. He knew how to use it because his stubborn godmother still had one.

"Hey, can I use your phone?"

She stared at the T.V. as a particularly exciting steamy scene was enfolding. She looked towards him and back to the television.

"Well, you charming lady, I'll take that as a yes." The scene ended, and she went to the bathroom in a rush.

He picked up the phone and called Carlos, each passing click of the dial causing Beto more pain and frustration.

"Hello," said a muffled voice.

"It's me," he said. "Are you okay?"

"Hello? Who is this? If it's you, I'm going to kick your ass next time I see you!"

"Hey!" said Beto. "It's me!"

Carlos paused and waited. At that point, the phone went dead.

The old woman came back hurried, plopping her posterior against the chair, just as her soap opera started again, and the protagonist shoved the man away in a final gesture of propriety.

"Your piece of junk phone doesn't work!" he yelled, as the woman analyzed every movement from the handsome co-star.

He stood exasperated, flailing his arms, but still, she didn't respond; he was about to pound his fist on the counter, when the T.V. grew snowy, and she adjusted the antenna.

She muttered, -Cosa malvada.-[4] She complained some more and snorted a juicy booger which she spat into a Kleenex.

"Seriously?" he left in a huff. This time, he walked taking in the town. It was quiet, he was sure because any sane person was indoors keeping cool. He wasn't sure what time it was, but he kept on walking. He went to the parish office and rang the bell. He rang several times before he realized no one was going to answer the door. After that, he tried the church, but the doors were locked.

---

[4] Evil thing.

He pounded his fist against the door, sending nesting birds away. The sidewalk was steaming, and the bag grew heavier with every step. He almost screamed as an enormous brown Doberman crossed his path. "Oh shit! Where'd you come from?"

The Doberman paused defying him.

"Good boy," Beto said in a soft voice.

The dog stared at him and started wagging its tail. Against better judgement, Beto reached out his hand, so the dog would smell him. It whimpered a pathetic plea. That's when he noticed the blood on the dog's back and right hind leg. It was crusted over, collecting flies.

"Hey, are you hurt buddy?"

The dog whined as Beto patted it on the head. Just then, the owner yelled for it, and the dog ran off on three legs, the fourth tucked at an awkward angle. He looked around for the owner, concerned, but the dog had gone back to the coolness of its home.

The walk back was less eventful than his dramatic jog to the church pantry. The sun was coming down, as he neared the altar for the second time. He paused again, adjusting the heavy grocery bag, and said another prayer, this time a heartfelt one.

"I'm so alone," he said to the universe. "And I need help."

A solitary dove landed on a plastic yellow rose on the cross and sang a desolate cry. He said, "You too, huh?" and it flew off into the distance.

He jogged back at a slow pace feeling the wind run through his wild hair. Disappointed that piece of crap rotary phone hadn't worked, Beto was determined to break into any home to use a phone, maybe even borrow one from a stranger. That's what he would do, stop at the corner store and borrow one from Big Lenny.

When Beto reached the corner store, everything was gloomy with that light before nightfall. The store would close by

7:00 p.m. because Big Lenny had another job at nearby Cocopah Casino.

"'Sup Lenny!" he said to his old friend.

Lenny was busy staring at a ledger. "It doesn't add up!" With a huff, he left to the back of the store.

Beto looked at the counter. There was a phone with an image of a naked woman as the screen saver.

"Big tits," he said out loud to no one. He picked up the phone and realized there was no security code.

He dialed his friend again. "Hello?" Carlos answered.

"Carlos! It's me, Beto!"

"Hello?"

A high-pitched sound made him drop the phone as Lenny returned.

"Fuck!" said Lenny.

"I'm sorry," said Carlos.

Lenny grabbed the phone as he sat in his dented leather seat and called someone. "Yo, Brian. I think Sheila's been stealing stock. Yeah. I know." He looked right at Beto and kept talking.

Beto said goodbye and left disappointed. It seemed like everyone was ignoring him. To punctuate his invisibility, while he was crossing the parking lot, an idiot in a red Ford almost ran him over. He came within inches of Beto and didn't even slow down.

He walked home faster. "To hell with everybody. I don't need you." As he sped past, the neighborhood dogs barked and howled. The wind began to pick up again, the sand darker and more ominous than before. He could see a few inches in front of him, but somehow, he made it home. When he neared the trailer, *he* was there again. This time he was sitting down on the steps, where Beto had sat so many nights waiting for his parents.

"Come with me," the man said.

Beto analyzed his face. He looked like a benevolent Jesus but with no beard.

"Where to?" he asked.

"Home."

"I am home."

"Open your eyes," he said and vanished.

Beto dropped the bag. The contents rolled in the sand. An orange reached the stairs where the man's foot had been. The bottom step was broken and when he walked into the trailer, it was a mess.

"What the hell?" All the furniture was missing.

"Damn that junkie!" he cried, blaming his neighbor. Or had the man done that? He sat and began to cry. As if feeling his sadness, his faithful friend came. Chuckey stopped at his feet as Beto cried in earnest. He petted the soft fur, and Chuckey began to howl.

"Stop that! Bad dog!" he said angrier than he intended. The dog yipped and ran off.

"I'm sorry! Come back!" But, Chuckey would never come back again.

THE BUCKET OF OLD BASEBALLS was in the back of the trailer. His mother admonished him for pitching against the trailer, but he had nowhere else to practice. He grabbed the reinforced plywood his father made for him, with metal sheets on the outside, and stood it against the trailer, securing it with large cement blocks. His father had painted concentric circles for him to aim at, which were almost perfect.

His vision was blurry from crying, but he stepped back far enough to challenge himself and threw the first pitch. His left shoulder ached, sharp like he had torn a ligament.

He told his shoulder, "What are you bothered for? You didn't do any work. You wussy shoulder, good for nothing, crying from carrying a bag."

He stopped and warmed up doing 20 jumping jacks and stretching out his arms, but the pain was still there.

"Who cares? I'm not on the team anymore anyway." He pitched rhythmically, speeding up with every throw, until the bucket was empty. He continued until he stopped crying and pitched the balls in succession three more times.

"I'm a bad ass," he said because every pitch had been fierce, and he hit every target he aimed for.

He relaxed his arm and readied to pitch his fastest fast pitch ever. But as he gripped the ball, he heard her scream again.

The ball slipped and aimed right for his bedroom window, shattering the cheap plastic. This time, there was something chilling about it, as the dogs began their sad song throughout the barrio.

BETO RAN to her house, without his bat or gun. It had been a protective instinct, thoughtless. He knew deep down something was wrong. Beto clambered over the gate and saw them struggling outside on the ground. At first, it appeared that he was pushing her down, but as he neared, he realized, her father was strangling her. He watched with horror as she turned a deep shade of pink.

"Get away from her!" he screamed. They were three yards away, but her father would not relent.

"NO!" Beto yelled as he ran towards them. That made her father pause, but he continued squeezing her neck.

His face was pure red, as he clamped down on her neck with extra effort. His blonde hair outlined his receding hairline. There was a rage of monsters on his face. Beto would never forget as the man grinned with effort. He ran towards her father bracing for impact. As he charged, Beto began to flail his arms. The vile man vanished like the dark stranger. He had to force himself to stop because the momentum carried him further than he wanted to go. He almost tripped as he spun around and ran back to her.

"No, no, no, no!" he cried, "Sarah, please wake up."

He put his head against her chest but heard and felt nothing. He kissed her face as she lay there, limp, cold. Her once rosy cheeks were a perpetual dark shade. He shook her, but nothing. He tried giving her mouth to mouth, but he knew she was gone. In a blink, she vanished.

He stood startled and called out her name. He spun around several times hoping to get more clarity.

In the distance, he saw black smoke rising from where his trailer was. He ran towards his trailer, and he saw her father moving frenetically around his home. Chuckey was barking at Mr. Stan who had a container of gasoline. The trailer was on fire. He neared and heard his parents screaming from inside but couldn't get out. This time Beto ran intent to kill him. He lunged, but went straight through, launching forward. Beto flew in what should have been his living room but landed on the ashen floor. He stood up stunned. Everything was gone. He stepped back and searched for them, even clawing at the ground, but they were nowhere.

"Chuckey?" No one answered.

He touched his hands to the floor or where the floor should have been. The ground was cool. Nothing made sense. He waited a few days before he went to see her again. Instead, he thought about the stranger. He wasn't a threat and just kept inviting him to go, but he could never leave her.

EIGHT DAYS LATER, when he reached her window, she was fast asleep again. "Man, girl, why are you so sleepy these days?" He smiled at her. "I'll give you something to be tired about. Just give me a chance."

He lay there, outside her bedroom window and stared at the stars. "62," he muttered to himself, "62 days that I come over, and I still don't have the balls to talk to you."

There had been plenty of opportunities. Sarah Stan was in his Spanish class. She had once been paired up with him, and he had sat there like a baboso mute on the street corner. Unable to even say, "Hola." The teacher never paired them up again.

Another time, she joined the church youth group. The group watched movies and on occasion played soccer. That day, that foolish Franciscan novitiate, Fred, had gotten inspired to have them read the Bible. Right in the middle of mispronouncing Ninevites with his thick beaner accent, she walked into the room. He stared unable to finish. The rest of group heckled him. Sarah smiled at him in that encouraging way, and he smiled an unimpressive smile, as he turned beet red and passed the book to the person next to him. He walked out never to return.

It was almost morning, and he decided to go back to the school, for no other reason than he was lonely and hoping Carlos would be practicing.

HE JOGGED AT A STEADY PACE. He didn't realize until 40 minutes later that he was running back to the locker room. He barged in almost knocking the old janitor over.

"Sorry!" he cried.

He went to his locker and sat in front of it catching his breath. He stared long and hard at it and began to notice the edges of notes and blurry pictures. He stared for a long time and thought back to a memory of his parents, and of Sarah Stan. She danced like a dervish in the middle of the dancefloor the first time he saw her.

His vision began to clear. In the center was an image that shocked and delighted him. It was an old Polaroid of her in his letterman jacket, the deep red and white jacket accentuating her delicate braid as he held her close. He was holding her, Sarah.

"What?" He tried reading the notes, but the words were blurry still. His head began to spin, and as he grew unsteady, he saw the man one more time.

"NO! I'M NOT GOING WITH YOU," he said and ran down the hall. He stopped before a make-shift altar and saw pictures of her and himself. There were candles and her favorite rainbow Tootsie rolls. He asked himself, *How did he know they were her favorite?*

"I'm having a dream," he said. He looked at all the pictures of his teammates. "Yeah, I'm dreaming." Deep down he knew that wasn't the case. What had the man said? *He had to see.*

He strained his eyes, but he still couldn't see anything. His coach appeared.

"What a damned shame," he said to no one.

"Hey," said Beto alarmed at hearing the man swear.

His coach said a long prayer, to Beto's surprise. "We all miss you Beto. You too, Sarah. I hope you both get some peace. *All* of you."

Beto waved in front of coach's face, but the coach didn't respond. "I'm right here!"

He walked away, as Beto stood there. He analyzed the table for a long time and after a while, calmed down.

We miss you! The words became clearer.

I hope your father burns in hell, Sarah! wrote someone in a deep angry black marker. Other angry messages followed and some sweet ones—*Be blessed in Heaven. Find peace, you two.*

He read message after message and began to remember.

They had been playing a rival team. They were down two runs, a player on first and second, and Beto re-experienced as the ball whizzed by a second time. The heat from the ball was amazing. He remembered as the pitcher had struck out Carlos and Peter both, so no one expected the team to win. In that instant, he saw her encouraging him. The pitcher threw his best curveball. Beto stepped in just at the right moment and swung so hard, when the bat connected, the ball went out of the park. He ran, as Sarah cheered for him in her immaculate uniform, getting out of formation. She bounced up and down, and he managed to grin at her as he ran past, and as he and his teammates made it home.

They won 7 to 6. Afterwards they had gone to Peter's house for an afterparty.

THAT FRIDAY NIGHT, they had been together, Beto and Sarah. They were celebrating the most astounding news, and stupid Peter had dared him to down four shots of tequila in quick succession. Sarah offered to drive, but he was macho; she kept insisting that he buckle up, if they were to have a future together, but he was fine. "I only had a few drinks," he slurred. Besides, he was taking his girl to a new spot.

"Wait until you see." He carried his mother's engagement ring in his left jean pocket, and he felt for it every now and then; a slim thing with a small ruby.

"Don't worry, baby. I'll take care of you." He had smiled as she grew more worried and bit the corner of her lip. He had kissed her as she flinched.

"You taste awful," she had said and kissed him again. He was rushing to get there as fast as possible. It was a sand dune that overlooked the valley, where no one else parked. She would love it.

When he hit 95 miles an hour in the dilapidated truck, something terrible happened. A dog like Chuckey ran in front of the truck, and he swerved, hitting a log that had no business being on the side of the road. The truck flipped, turning his world upside down. As he reached for her, his head snapped to the right and left. His left shoulder screamed as a hateful metal claw crushed it. Glass shot at his face embedding in his eyes and soft places. He relived her screams, Sarah crying out for him, a terrifying Nightling shriek, as the world went dark.

That was it. There was no light at the end of the tunnel. No angelic music greeting him to the other side. The next day, he woke up at his empty trailer. His parents were gone, and he didn't know where they went. All that mattered was seeing her because he loved her beyond life.

He held his breath for a long time.

"I'm dead," he said.

How could he be dead? He had talked to people! Gone to the pantry. Yet, not everyone had seen him, not even Coach, and he was never one to prank anyone.

"Come with me," said the man. He was standing right next to him like Carlos would before a big game, side by side for moral support.

50

Beto turned to look at him—a deep burning rage incubating in his chest. "I'm not going without her. *Ever.* Do you understand?"

He whispered, "She also cannot see; thus, she cannot leave."

"What happened to her?" he asked, but the man didn't add any details.

Beto stared at the man and sized him up. "You taking me to hell?"

The man smiled and beckoned.

"I'll take that as a, 'No'. Where are my parents?"

But again, the man was silent.

The heat emanated through his body. "That fucking asshole of her father. If he had been more tolerant, none of this would have happened. It's his fault!"

Beto took a look at the elaborate altar again. There was an article about her, dated June 10. He read at a rate his honor's English teacher would have been proud of and soaked in every choppy paragraph.

She had survived the crash, and in a fit, her piece of shit racist father had strangled her. His heart froze. He read on.

"It's my fault she's dead. Her and my son," he said to no one. "My parents, too."

That evil man did deserve to go to hell. Everyone had always said so, and they were right. Beto would get that son of a bitch, even if it meant haunting him for eternity.

WHEN HE REACHED HER WINDOW, the moon was out. He called out her name, but she was fast asleep. In the distance, her furious father was screaming at someone.

He was dead, Beto was sure of it. Or maybe it was a memory she couldn't get out of. She was in a loop of hate, made by that terrible so-called man, but Beto would wake her.

Beto remembered that she cherished his singing, even though Beto couldn't sing to save his life. As he stood outside her window, he sang her an old corrido about two lovers who committed suicide. At first his song was soft, but it grew louder. The song ended, and he waited for what seemed an eternity. Just as he was about to sing another song, her lights turned on, and she looked out the window.

"Sarah," he called out. She smiled at him that amazing smile, just for him. *God how he wanted to kiss that mouth forever.*

She came out the front door and ran to him like old times. She wrapped her arms around him, rubbing her fingers on the back of his neck that sent chills through his core.

"Beto! Where have you been? I've been so worried!"

"I'm so, so sorry," he said in the most sincere and pathetic tone.

"For what?" She smiled at him.

He took her by the hand away from that hate-filled place. Away from that degenerate Mexican-hating father who didn't deserve to share the same planet as his Sarah.

"Where are we going?" she asked.

They walked for a long time until they reached the side of the road with the yellow roses.

"You remember this place?" he asked.

She looked around and nodded. She said, "We crashed here. It was the worst night of my life."

"I'm so sorry," he said taking her in his arms and holding her tight.

"But, you're okay!" she said. Sarah punched him in the arm. "I could never be mad at you." She looked into his eyes uncertain, a memory tugging at her.

In the far distance, two figures approached, but he had no time for them. He reached into his pocket, and there it was. He looked at her, straight into those eyes he adored, and slipped the humble ring on her finger. "It's too late for us, but I want us to be together. Somehow. I think we can be."

The radiance in her face diminished. "Why? Don't you want to marry me? I thought you didn't want to live in sin or whatever. I told you we should have run off to Vegas. Is this because of Dad? To hell with him Beto. We can make it."

"Of course, sweetie, but I'm dead." He looked into her eyes and waited for her to understand. "And so are you. We're not running anywhere. Not Vegas. Not city hall."

She stared stunned. "What?" Sarah laughed that laugh that made her entire body shake.

"You were pregnant," he said choking down a sob. "Remember? I got drunk because I was going to ask you for your hand, and after, I was going to ask your crazy dad to his face. Remember?"

Sarah analyzed her abdomen. He saw it, that intelligent sparkle in her eye. She stopped breathing, placing her hands over her belly. Beto was certain. Sarah could see.

Beto held onto her, as he saw the brutal bruises emerge on her neck again. She began to gasp for air arching her rigid body.

"No, no! Come back!" Part of Beto began to die with her as pure rage imbued him. Every gasp of pain struck at his soul. Her suffering lasted a few minutes, and he was grateful for at least that much.

Beto focused his pain and hatred on her father. He thought, "That bastard. I will never, ever forgive him."

She lay lifeless, as he cradled her, and once again, he kissed her face and prayed for her to return. He imagined himself having to sing at her window, night after night for all time. Sarah, just a glass pane away from freedom. He would sing until they could be together again and liberate her.

Maybe, he should have been more tactful, but he was tired. Tired of walking around with no one to talk to. Tired of missing his parents. Tired of living an illusion. Tired of not remembering her. What they had was near-perfect. *How could he have forgotten her?* For Beto, that was worse than hell.

He held her as the two figures grew closer. He began to sing to her again as he traced his lips down her neck.

"Come on Sarah. We're supposed to be together for always. Para siempre, remember?" He sang and struggled through his tears and ran songs together that made no sense.

This time, her eyes fluttered.

"I remember." She began to sob and paused wide eyed. She looked at her abdomen. "Where's the baby?"

Beto looked towards the figure. "I think he's home. Waiting for us. . . . Probably being spoiled by my mom." He smiled, as she pecked him below the chin.

"I'm not leaving your side," she said. "Not ever."

"Same, Sweet Sarah." That's what he used to call her.

He recalled everything now.

When he got the news at the end of spring, he had been so overjoyed, not terrified as others might be. Yet, he had been so foolish because he hadn't needed courage to confront her father. He could stand on his own, and he was more of a man than Mr. Stan would ever be, that piece of human garbage.

He thought, *Had he been any better?*

Beto had been *monumentally* stupid. Still, as he held her, none of that mattered now. He had no room for hate or regret. All that remained was them, and not even death or her stupid raging father could take that away. Still, he couldn't help hating the man and wanting to beat him to a pulp with his bat. He held her too tight as he imagined bludgeoning him, his head becoming a mass of soup. He sneered breathing in some of her hair.

She gasped. "You're crushing me."

He loosened his grip a bit and kissed her one last time as he looked up. The two approaching figures were so much alike, thin and expressionless, like a stereotype of death, two skinny white dudes with deadpan faces.

"Ah," said the new stranger, "thank you Alberto Andrades. Sarah's eyes are open now."

"She couldn't have seen without you," said the companion.

Beto smiled. "She's my girl. She will always be my girl." The second man gave him a sullen stare and turned his back.

"Are you ready to come home?" The other one asked her. She looked from him to Beto. "Your child is waiting for you."

She asked Beto. "Who are they?"

"I think they're like tour guides to Heaven." He looked at the expansive horizon. "I'll guess we'll find out together. What do you say, my Sweet Sarah? Should we follow these two white dudes, you and me?"

He giggled and nodded her head.

Sarah stepped forward and asked one of them, "Will my baby really be there?" The other Dark Puto nodded, as he reached out his arm as a prom date would, leading her through the gym doors, and then, the other Puto did the same. She turned back, smiling just for him as they guided her away. Beto beamed back, his chest puffed out, happy to be with her again.

A few seconds later they were a quarter of a mile away, as he lagged behind. They grew further away, while Beto was no longer the fastest runner, his feet sticking to the sand. Beto tried to gain on them with all of his might but fought to keep up. He would near them, and just as he was about to touch her, they moved further way.

Why weren't they taking him with them? Every muscle in his body screamed. The palpable rage—that unforgiveness—implanted itself in his heart again.

This was all that bastard's fault. He killed her! He killed them. He deserved to go to hell. No. Worse. He was the one who should wander the earth alone and forgotten. . . . And that piece of shit Peter, with his damned shots of tequila, needed to meet Anti-Puto and suffer. He should have been the one to die in that car crash, over and over!

Beto's body grew more sluggish as he cursed and cried, "Sarah!" She was too far away to hear him now, and as she departed, he was struck at her beautiful hair flowing in the wind.

"Wait!" he cried a high-pitched mournful howl that rose to the cruel sky, and the barrio dogs accompanied him, while Sarah Isabelle Stan finally walked home.

Magical Bully

Rita Sifuentes was sitting at her outdated Dell computer while most kids her age were watching YouTube or sleeping in on a Saturday morning. She frowned, turning her cheek in that funny backwards Y.

"Come on stupid thing! Load faster!" Rita hit the monitor. Her long obsidian black hair was an increasing nuisance that kept getting in her face, even with it tied back. Somehow, strands managed to escape the tightest ponytail. She looked down at her legs. Her long lanky body was a barrio joke in the desert of Nopales, Arizona. The other kids would call her noodle or worse, lombriz—tapeworm. The kids in her neighborhood were just jealous of her. At least, that's how she saw it. She was getting out of the barrio, and they were not.

She was the only one with a computer, although it was three years old, ancient by modern standards. By her recollection, she was the only ninth-grader in her neighborhood who had won first place in the science fair. Rita had also won first place in the math bowl, to the acid hatred of the junior and senior nerds. Her Nana didn't know what to make of all the ribbons with the cryptic writing hanging all over the house, but she was proud of her Rita.

Her Nana was a bent reed with long bright white hair like the clouds on a hot summer day. Her abuelita would wear it in a lengthy silky braid, and whenever the kids would come outside their fence and make fun of Rita, she would chase after them with her cane, shouting -¡Cállensen canijos!-[5] When her parents weren't home, Nana would chuck rocks at them. Once when Lizandro called her a puta, a whore, her Nana let out Bucho. In truth, Bucho, wouldn't hurt a fly, but it was a large Rottweiler. It would just get excited to see other kids, so it would bark a low bark and prance after them. Once, Lizandro got so scared that his feet tangled up. He fell down. Busted his front teeth. And never called Rita any bad names. At least not to her face and never in front of her house.

Rita sighed a long sigh. At last, the web site she had been waiting for loaded. She had become intrigued by homemade products and their implications in a consumer economy. Her economics teacher, Mr. Levy, a leftist hiding in a conservative school, encouraged her to do so. He would give her easy articles and even loaned her a book about Marx.

"Look at the bibliography and get the good books at the public library," he whispered in her ear. "We'll email each other to talk about the books." Most of the time, she understood the introduction before getting stuck, but it was a start, and she always had good online chats with her teacher.

She once had a secret crush on Mr. Levy who was 23, close enough for her to imagine possibilities. She was fourteen, and it might have worked, if she hadn't discovered him kissing his partner, Enrique, the music teacher, after school. That was her first encounter with homosexuals besides her father heckling and taunting the jotos[6] in San Luis, the Mexican border town. She had been so shocked, she crept back out like a mime in a French movie. She wanted to scream. But, she was an open-minded girl, and she never told anyone. Not even her Nana.

But that was all in the past, and now she was great friends

---

[5] Shut up, jerks!
[6] Gays

with Mr. Levy and Mr. Gill. They had her over for dinner sometimes, when her parents had to drive her Nana to the doctor in San Luis.

A few weeks ago, she heard that Mr. Gill was breaking out. She wanted to show her appreciation of their generosity, so she was looking up homemade beauty products. Mr. Gill was having allergic reactions to something. She wanted to make him a natural astringent and a scrub, maybe even soap. She scanned the web site and found other products, homemade lip balm and shampoo. She would start with the scrub.

Most of the items were in the desert. She could use aloe for the shampoo and fine sand for the scrub. She decided to make the scrub that morning, so she went out to collect some unique sand.

It was 11:00 a.m. The sun would be in full force within the hour, but Rita was used to the heat. She took an old bottle of water and put on generous sunscreen lotion. On her way out, her Nana put a large hat on her head.

-Mija, ten cuidado con los duendes,- warned Nana. Her wise grandmother was always warning her about the *Little People*. Her grandmother warned her about La Llorona, the Crying Woman who kidnapped children near bodies of water. Rita had to watch out for The Devil, the *literal* Devil. But her grandmother wasn't so concerned about him because Rita was obedient and only went out in the daytime like good girls were supposed to. Duendes, on the other hand, were a constant concern for her Nana.

Duendes were lost souls of naughty children who did not make it to Purgatory. Unbaptized children who managed to beat the system. Somehow, they had remained on earth to continue their pranks. Rita nodded in agreement, just to please her old Nana.

Ever since Rita could understand words, her Nana would tell her the most incredible stories. She was convinced duendes would steal the chickens, even though the desert abounded with coyotes. She would tell her stories of flying witches and ghosts who would kidnap children. As a young child, it used to frighten Rita to the point that she would pee her pants, but when she started reading books, she realized they were just stories that many people told to frighten or fascinate.

-Si Nana. No se preocupe,- she replied and meant it. She would never cause her family trouble or worry.

Her Nana said, -Si vez a un duende, jálale los oídos para que te deje en paz y échale un pedo en la cara.- Rita bit down on her tongue. She could imagine herself warding off Little People by yanking tiny ears and farting in their faces. What a scene that would make! Rita walked out in the steaming desert. She could feel the energy seeping out, but she willed her body to move forward.

"Bucho, let's go boy." Bucho bounded towards her. It licked her leg and gave its low bark. She opened the back gate and headed for the part of the desert where the sand changed. It was a different texture than all the rest of the sand. Once she had asked the science teacher to analyze it for chemicals, like the ones the chickens had drunk from the barrels left by some stranger. Some chickens died just from stepping on the red mess. She couldn't figure out what would make the sand different. The wind blew the same over it. The same shrubs grew around it, but it was made of smaller whiter sand particles. Almost as white as beach sand from the postcards in the pharmacy.

"Bucho, be careful of rattle snakes." Bucho barked in acknowledgement.

She realized, she had no container, so she turned back and grabbed a jar that was drying in the sun. It was one of the jars her mom used to pickle nopales, flat cactus. Her mami would sell the jars at the Swap Meet to faded retired ladies and their husbands.

She walked and walked until she reached the spot. Something in the sand swirled. She stepped back looking around for Bucho. But it was busy barking down a jackrabbit hole.

"Your eyes are playing tricks on you." She eyed the spot, but it was still. She dipped her jar into the sand with care, as she would pet an injured animal. It felt oily to her fingers, which was odd. *Was the sand contaminated? Was it bleached out by human machinations?* she wondered.

Again, the sand moved in a gentle swirl. "Gopher?" She hypothesized. A green thing poked up from the sand. Rita screamed. Bucho was no coward and ran straight toward her at incredible speed. It barked at the green form, and the creature slipped back under the sand. Rita was not a biologist, but she knew there were no green animals like that in the desert. Bucho calmed down, and she observed the sand a while longer. A few yards away lay a long thin stick. Rita mustered her courage, grabbed the stick, and poked where the green thing had been.

"Ouch!"

Rita jumped back dropping her jar. Bucho began barking again.

"It's bad enough you're taking my house apart without you nearly poking my eye out!" said an angry muffled voice.

"Holy shit!" Rita was curious, and as the annual science fair winner, she sort-of knew a great discovery when she poked one. But she wasn't about to hang around. The barrio girl in her told her to get the heck out of there! She grabbed her jar and hightailed it to her house with Bucho running after her—for moral support, of course. When she ran inside the gate, she found her parents home from work after a long morning of picking lettuce. This was unusual and meant the fields were being inspected. They were wearing soaked red handkerchiefs over their head. Their denim pants were brown from the wind blowing sand at them.

Her father smiled a warm smile at her, but her mother scowled. "What are you doing running in this heat, mija? You'll get dehydrated! And look at poor Bucho. Give him some water. Wait. What's in that jar? You don't have a scorpion or a tarantula in there do you?"

Rita couldn't speak, but she shook her head. Her mother, Amparo, nodded and went into the house with a, "I hope you got your chores done before you ran off like a wild Arab."

Rita rolled her eyes, and her father chuckled. He understood why Rita didn't like racist jokes, just like he hated the gringo bosses joking about Mexicans during their lunch hour. They were no more than *greasers* and *wetbacks* to them.

Her father gave her a concerned look. "What happened mija? Were you outrunning another rattle snake?"

Rita shook her head. "Papi, I think I saw a duende." Her papi looked at her and paled a little.

"Come on mija," he stammered. "There are no duendes in America. No one believes in them anymore. Besides, they hate technology." He eyed the horizon.

"Papi, we live in the desert."

Her father patted her head and began to walk inside the house. "Well did you pull its ears?"

She shook her head. "No Papa; it was under the sand."

Taking his hat and slapping it against his thigh, he said, "¡Carajo! I'll tell your Nana to put protection around the house. ¡Que lata!"[7]

At one level, Rita couldn't believe what had just happened. At another, she also couldn't believe her father didn't think she was nuts or hallucinating from the heat. Fast as a road runner, she

---

[7] What a drag!

watered Bucho and gave it a good soak. It gave her a grateful bark and a lick on the left knee. Rita looked out into the distance. Her senses were more alert than the time she shook a scorpion off her leg. In the horizon, she was sure she saw a pointed green hat. The figure was too dark for her to discern what it was, but that was enough.

When she walked inside, her mother and father were arguing. Clearly, her mother's grandmother had not told her mom many cuentos, fairy tales, or gossip about supernatural occurrences.

"Oh, for Pete's sake!" she exclaimed.

"Blasfemia, Amparo," muttered Nana.

"Oh, but believing in fairy folks is not? Come on Patricio! She is still impressionable. Oh, for the love of God, what is Nana doing with that holy palm and onions?" Her husband shrugged his shoulders, bowed his head, and walked to the kitchen to warm up food, thought better of it, and headed for the shower instead.

Her Nana marched outside and went about her business, as if there was nothing unusual in the matter. Rita had never been more grateful to be in their tiny brick home with faded lime walls. Her mother looked at her and at her husband. No one took her side, and she headed for the shower in disgust. Rita went to the kitchen; it was connected to the living room.

Somehow, the maestro who built the house forgot to put in a dining room. That made for a very cramped cooking and dining space in an already crowded house. Not wanting to upset her mother anymore, Rita helped by peeling and chopping the remaining onions. While she was crying and cutting away, her Nana marched in and snagged a couple more onions. She winked at Rita.

A few minutes later, her mother walked in wearing a thin

dress and towel on her head. Her mom was used to taking fast showers, if she ever got the chance to come home. She stood imposing, looking at the old woman. For her part, Nana averted her daughter-in-law's look of disgust.

-Esa tierra es buena y curativa,- said her grandmother pointing at Rita's jar which rested on the kitchen table. The sand had healing powers, according to Nana, which might explain how the green thing could live under it. Rita put her fingers to her temple to counter an emerging headache.

Rita asked out loud, "How could it speak under the sand? How could it *breathe* under the sand?"

She wondered why she never noticed the creature before, when she nicked her middle finger. "Ouch!"

Her mother gave her a disapproving look. "Pay attention! Rinse the finger off and put some Neosporin on it. Now."

Rita went to the main bathroom with the sand in hand. "Hmm, let's put Nana's theory to the test. After all, my teacher assured me that natural dirt was clean, right?"

She rinsed her hand off and washed it with soap. Next, she covered the little cut with sand. It bled way too much for a nick, but the sand made it stop. The band-aid she surrounded the cut with fit just right. Not too tight, not too loose.

She returned to the kitchen to a command.

"Mija, watch the sopa," her mother ordered.

Her mama was frying the pasta for their soup and passed the chore onto Rita. This was one of the responsibilities besides cutting that Rita was allowed. Her mother thought she was still too young to cook, but the truth was that her Nana would let her do everything when her mom was not around. In fact, most of the time she and Nana did the house chores together, so Rita could spend more time on schoolwork. Sometimes, during finals, Nana would do *all* the chores. The one thing Rita could not make was tamales, but someday she would. Rita browned the pasta and added the tomato sauce. Her mom came in time to do the rest.

"Here, Rita. Taste."

"Needs salt and more garlic salt, but it has plenty of consomé."[8] Rita smiled at her mom, and her mom gave her a hug. That was their way of making peace. Her mom could never stay angry. None of them could.

Her mother said, "Your Nana sure is nutty sometimes. But we have to humor old folks just like children. After all, we will grow old someday. If God wills it."

Rita smiled, noticing the brown splotches on her mother's beautiful withering face. Her eyes were an unusual grey, and she had the same annoying long hair peppered with silver that her mother called highlights. She was thin, which brought the scorn and envy of many of her friends. To Rita, her mother was a queen, too gorgeous to be slaving in the sun.

Her father walked in refreshed and sat at the small table. She looked at her father who was sitting and reading the news on his phone. -¡Mira pues![9]- he would say without explaining. Unlike her taller fair skinned mother, he was a few inches shorter than her mother with tan skin and warm brown eyes. He was chato; thick curls and flat-nosed. His ears were delicate and small like the European ears her mother and she both envied.

Nana came back looking like she was going out on a date. She always looked her best before eating lunch or dinner and claimed her guardian angel instructed her to do so.

They all sat in harmony, as her father gave a short grace and ate the feast of rice and shredded chicken tacos. "Who made the

---

[8] Bouillon
[9] Look here!

65

tacos?" he asked. The three women all claimed the culinary victory, and another amicable battle of words ensued.

LATER THAT NIGHT, Nana put extra onion peels around the window. She came to her room to tuck her in with the pungent smell of onions sticking to her thick brown blanket.

-¿Porque no les gusta la cebolla a los duendes?- Nana had never explained why duendes hated stinky odors.

Her Nana smiled at her and elaborated that duendes had very particular senses of smells. Anything unpleasant would send them running away. Rita laughed at this idea.

Her Nana pinched her nose and told her, -Le deberías de haberle echado un pedo.-[10] Rita giggled unable to stop. -No te rías, es grave-,[11] her Nana said in a stern Spanish. Rita almost peed herself.

Nana continued, -Ahora ese enano verde bastardo va ha pensar que le tienes miedo. Volverá para hacerte la vida cuadritos.-[12]

Rita froze. It was bad enough being teased by all the boys. She didn't need some supernatural creature joining the bandwagon. Nana nodded understanding her plight and continued, -Yo se. Antes yo también era una miedosa, pero tu padre. ¡Ijuela, como era cobarde!-[13]

"Tell me the story. You've never told me this one." She begged.

Nana was about to tell the story when her father walked in. He said, -Buenas Noches, mi vida.-[14]

---

[10] You should have farted at it.

[11] This is no laughing matter.

[12] Now that little green bastard will think you are afraid of it. It might come back to pick on you.

[13] I know. I was a frightened girl once too, but your father! Oh boy was he a coward!

Nana clammed up and kissed Rita on the forehead. -La mano.-

Rita responded, -Dios la haga una santa. . . . La mano.-

Her Nana smiled. -Dios te haga una Santa.-

They always said the same thing at night—*The Hand. God make you a saint. The Hand. God make you a saint.*

-Después de que te empiece a joder, va ha hacerte mas santa con el sufrimiento,-[15] Nana said bringing a chill down Rita's spine. "You fight," said her elder in broken English.

Rita was always pleased when her grandmother spoke English. She rarely did because she had such a heavy accent, but Rita loved to hear her grandma say things to her. Rita was the one with whom Nana spoke English which made it special.

Rita smiled despite her plight. "I love you Nana."

Nana gave her a loving pinch.

Patricio looked at his daughter wiping his brow with an old kerchief. "Mija, if you want, you can sleep with the light on tonight. La Jefa says it's okay. We can let Bucho into the house, too. Remember to be brave. They can't hurt you. But you can hurt yourself if you don't think with your coco."[16] He knocked on his head with a fist.

Bucho was never allowed inside the house, unless she was alone with Nana, and her parents were on a rare vacation. On normal occasions, that would have been a treat. Now, his sanctioned presence increased her fear. *What possible taunting could the duende do? Why was her Papi so afraid of the duende when Nana was not?*

Bucho trotted into her bedroom with an onion necklace

---

[14] "Good night, my life" is a term of endearment.

[15] Although after this thing taunts you, you very well may become holier from the suffering

[16] Coco is a slang term for head.

around its neck. It woofed at Rita and jumped on the tiny bed.

"Holy cow, you stink!" It gave her a slapping lick and made himself comfortable. "Bucho! You're hogging the bed!" She struggled to push it against the wall.

Finally, Rita was comfortable, as comfortable as one could be with the heavy onion smell. She went to bed dreaming of grilled onions and huge pizzas that rolled around singing love songs to the clouds. *When the moon becomes round like a big pizza pie that's amore.* It was a funny dream, and she couldn't help but laugh until she woke herself up.

The moon was a large lover's lantern that night. She looked around the room and made out shapes in the shadows for fun. There sat an old woman knitting a scarf. There was a maiden with long wavy hair. A beaker floated above her head but vanished in a sheet of black.

As she began to doze off, a large form overshadowed her. Bucho stood on the bed growling at the small window. Rita looked outside, and she saw a fuzzy form. She stared at it. She thought it was one of the goats gone loose looking into the window, but soon, two electric blue eyes peered at her. No goat had eyes like that. A face emerged between a sheet of hair. It was paste pale and had long hair all the way to its feet. The duende was the size of a toddler and fit in the window. But it was *not* a child. Its body was thick, with the features of an older man.

That night the duende was wearing purple or what looked like purple with glitter stripes. It smiled at her and started to make obscene gestures. Then, it turned around, bent over, and pulled down its cute festive pants.

This upset Rita far more than her earlier encounter with the creature. No one had been so rude to her as to pull down his pants. The duende turned around without pulling its pants up, and that was more than Rita could handle. Yes, it was definitely NOT a child. She hid below the window and ran to her bed. "Pinche pervert."[17]

She went back to bed, and Bucho started barking like it wanted to tear something apart. The duende was gone. She began to relax, when its creepy head started to slink up the window. The duende was now stark naked, and it was picking its nose like a champion. It took a green mess from its nose and smeared, "U R A Ugly lizard," on the window.

This offense and the grammar error were more than she could handle. "I'm an ugly lizard?" Without thinking Rita put a chair below the window, so her butt could be in full view of the little jerk. She opened the window, turned around, and bent over hoping she could fart a tremendous explosion.

To her surprise, a mere squeak came out. It was pathetic. The church mice could fart louder than that. She turned to see the reaction of the duende. He was laughing and rolling around in the air, until he caught the faintest whiff and disappeared. There was no smoke, no sound. It just vanished and didn't return. Rita was so angry at her inability to outdo the duende with nastiness that she got no sleep the rest of the night.

The next day Rita went to school bleary-eyed and tired, even more exhausted than when she woke up at 4:00 a.m. to help her mother make tamales on holidays. During math she fell asleep and hit her head against the desk. The whole class laughed like a bunch of loud cackling chickens. The math teacher, not wanting to reprimand his favorite student, sent her to the library. There, she found an empty corner and fell asleep over a large dictionary. She woke up to a fluttering noise. She looked up and saw the librarian, Ms. Scott, who had a look of horror on her face. She was a large soft woman with fiery red hair and moss green eyes. The times she had

---

[17] Damned pervert.

seen her, Ms. Scott had a smile on her face, but today there was a storm swirling in her eyes. Rita looked down to see if she had drooled on the book. Instead she found hundreds of little Post-its stuck everywhere. They were fixed all over her body. Tiny neat handwriting was in each one of the notes.

Slut, ugly, stupid, skinny, dumb, crazy, fea—ugly, again. The last one hurt the most. On and on the insults went. Ms. Scott was furious.

"Who did this to you!" She demanded. Before Rita could answer, Ms. Scott grabbed her by the arm and led her to the principal's office. A massive blob stuck to her with a silly string hanging after it.

The principal was not in, so the vice principal, Ms. Morris, was called in to assess the situation. The counselor, Mr. Ortega, came in soon afterwards. The three authority figures were trying to coax the truth out of her.

"Honestly!" Rita replied. "I was fast asleep. I didn't get any sleep last night, so my teacher sent me to study hour to take a nap."

The three looked at her in disbelief. Ms. Morris tried to call her parents, but they were out slaving in the fields, and Nana pretended not to speak English when she answered the phone for fear of telemarketers. After ten minutes of getting nowhere, they removed the notes from her and sent her back to Mr. Levy's class. When Rita walked into the classroom, Mr. Levy gave her a worried look. Someone had called him on the phone on her way to math class.

He said, "Class open your books to chapter twelve, do a brief outline of the contents, and ask questions on the reading material."

"On math?" groaned Lizandro. "It sucks."

The room roared with laughter.

"Do you want a pop quiz?" spat Mr. Levy. Silence and

compliance followed.

Rita had done her homework the day before. She pulled it out of her desk and handed it to Mr. Levy.

Levy whispered, "What happened? Are you okay? Tell me who put all those degrading insults on you."

Rita choked and answered, "I didn't see who did it." That was not a lie, but she had a prime suspect.

Levy handed her a paper. "It's something I'm submitting to a journal. Check it out. It's an analysis of agri-business and its effects on women of color in the Southwest."

Rita nodded. She could tell him in one sentence what agri-business did to her mother—It was giving her chronic back pain and arthritis for a ridiculous wage. She went back to her desk and proceeded to read the paper. Levy kept looking at her, which made Rita blush. She didn't like people staring at her too long, and some of the students were already glancing at her. Gossip would follow.

The counselor walked into the classroom unexpectedly and handed something in a folder over to Mr. Levy. Levy analyzed the contents with great scrutiny and indicated, "No." Rita figured they wanted to know who put the Post-its all over her. The counselor walked back out. Poof. Vanished. Just like the duende.

Levy gave her one last searching look and turned away to reprimand Arnulfo for shooting a spit wad at Jenny Peterson's long blonde hair. The rest of the period went by as she read page after page of the article. In truth, it was very interesting.

She made a few minor corrections on his use of Spanish and handed the paper back to Levy when the final bell rang. "Here. I made a few corrections. Tu Español vale madre.[18] And I agree with you completely. Women are underpaid and undervalued. . . . You use too many big words for a paper about simple women."

---

[18] Your Spanish sucks.

"But they're not so simple," he said winking at her. She smiled and walked away with a spring in her walk.

Levy's class was the last one of the day. Now came the torture of riding in the over-crowded bus. No one ever let her sit with them, and she wasn't allowed to stand up, so she would have to wait for the second bus. She hated riding the bus and wished she were old enough to drive. She walked to the curb and was surprised to see her father there.

"Hola mija!" She ran up to him unworried about her reputation and hugged him. He explained that he had asked the boss to let him go before the end of his shift. "Family emergency," he had pleaded. He never asked for time off, and his foreman was feeling generous that day.

It was another warm day, and the busted air conditioning in her dad's old Ford truck never worked. She didn't mind so much, and her father managed to get a few laughs from her.

"Today, Venancio found a surprise in his sandwich."

"Oh?" she asked with enough curiosity to coax out the rest of the story.

"Well, he had packed a ham sandwich with jalapenos, and he got a little extra something. He took a big bite and was having a hard time chewing it. So, he looked inside. . . ."

Rita groaned, "Apa. Is this another mouse in the torta story?"

"No'mbre! This really happened! He was chewing and chewing, so Paco said, '¿Pues que chingados tienes?'[19] So Venancio looked inside, and he had bitten the head off a lizard!"

"Gross!"

Her father added, "It was one of the little blue ones, and he pulled it out with the little dangly tail. Everyone laughed so hard!

---

[19] What the hell is wrong with you?

Even your mother laughed when she found out."

Rita smiled at her father. He was red from working in the sun. So red he could have been the brunt of bad indio jokes. That rouge never left him, and she worried that he would get skin cancer. "Who put it in there?"

"Well, nobody from work. Probably his wife. He cheated on her again with that fake blonde lady. What's her name?"

"La Chueca?"

"Yeah. That's the one. It probably managed to get in and suffocated from the sandwich or Venancio's awful body odor." He laughed again at his own wit. "Did I tell you the one—"

"Yes." It was the same joke he told her on rides home. One day Venancio put his work boots on in the morning. What he didn't know was that there was a black widow in the left boot. Sadly, there was a tragic death. . . . The poor spider died from the stench.

"Well, truthfully, nobody knows how the lizard got in there. Kind of like nobody knows how Jesus fed all those people. It just happened. Maybe a duende put it in there!"

Rita didn't laugh. It was a common expression. A duende did this or that mischief.

Patricio looked at her stern face and apologized. "Aye mija. I'm sorry. I forgot. Hey, let's go for a ride in the desert. That will cheer you up."

Patricio took a detour and raged across the sand. It was his favorite pastime to speed up and try to run over the gophers. Those vermin would ruin the dirt borders around the fields and kill the crops, most of all the vulnerable seedlings. Less crops meant less money. Rita would always protest in defense of the gophers, but he never got one. At least there was never any evidence on the tires.

This time, his daughter wasn't laughing like she always did.

"You know what would cheer me up?" she said. "I want to

hear about your duende story."

"Oh, then we would both be ready for a funeral with our sad faces. Some other time, huh? When you graduate from community college."

"University."

"Colegio."

"Universidad."

Her father insisted, "Silver Community College. Why do you need to go so far?"

"University! Don't change the subject."

They went on until the gophers ran out. He headed home and took one last detour to a puesto, a family-owned stand, where they sold raspados[20] and lemon water.

They sat down on the old aluminum table with the beat-up umbrella. Rita was determined to hear the story, but she wasn't pushing her luck. One prod too many, and her father would avoid the subject.

"Okay. I'll tell you the highlights like in the World Cup, except not so loud."

Rita smiled. The highlights would mean no embellishment, something most Mexican parents she knew were good at. Not her dad, but then, she reconsidered.

"Apa." She cleared her throat, "It would be better if I knew as much as possible."

He nodded and continued, "Okay, when I was eight years old, and your Nana was a foxy lady, we used to live in a rancho away from the pueblo. You went there when you were teeny tiny, but you don't remember. Anyway, I used to tend the goats until late at night. I was a brave boy in the dark because if I didn't, your Nana would hit me with a stick. She was mean. Not nice like she is with

---

[20] Flavored shaved ice

you. Consentida."[21]

Rita smiled. She was Nana's favorite, but she had no siblings to compete with, and no more were coming any time soon.

"One night, my Papa took a long time to come get me. I was out alone at night, resting under an old tree. It's not there anymore because your Nana chopped it down with a machete, by herself. Anyway, I saw a pair of fiery green eyes. At first, I thought it was a bruja. But no. It was a duende, with brown skin and white silvery hair. It was mad because I had torn a branch off his tree. What did I know? I was just a kid. There were no toys to play with out there. But it was angry! It started chasing after me, so I ran, leaving the goats behind." Patricio hit the side of his leg.

"Boy did I catch hell from my parents when I got home without the goats. But I was so scared, I couldn't say anything. My dad got worried because I just stood there like a big dummy. He got his shotgun and came to where the goats were. When we got there, the damned duende had given the goats bad haircuts. All of them. Some of them had crazy flower patterns. Others had bad words shaved all over them. The next day, I was the laughing stock of all the goat herders. Well, all the herders. They thought I did it. That I was sick in the coco. Things just got worse from that day.

"The worst thing was that the damned duende dyed all my clothes pink. My parents couldn't afford new clothes and didn't know how to take the damned pink out. We didn't have bleach in those days, so I had to go to school looking like a girl. That did it.

"One day, I went to the tree and had a big standoff. I yanked its ears and did everything short of shitting on it. It never bothered me again, and it moved away. Your Nana chopped the tree down because she didn't want any more duendes to move in. She used the wood for firewood. That firewood was magic, mija. It lasted

---

[21] Favored

75

almost fifteen years. We never thought to make a tea out of it, but your Nana did accidentally when some of the wood fell into the tea pan, and after that it became the magic cure for stomachaches and ear infections.

"You know, if I had been braver sooner, I wouldn't have suffered so much. No one can be brave for you chula. You have to do it on your own, see? Nana couldn't do it for me, and neither could my father. They went looking for the duende, but he would never appear for them. Eventually, you will have to stand up to it, but it will have to be when you are ready. You have to have big balls or get really mad."

Rita smiled at her father. "Or grow ovaries and get *really* mad." They chuckled then laughed out loud. She could stand up for herself. This time she couldn't rely on her Nana, but she wasn't about to go there without reinforcements of some kind. "What if I take the sand back? Did you try giving the branch back?"

"No. But it wouldn't have mattered. I don't think. Imagine if I would get so angry that I would chase a man down with a gun if he came and took a little bit of junk from the scrap heap in the backyard. You would call the police and send me to the manicomio[22] to get wrapped up in one of those tight white jackets." He pretended to be tied down with his arms wrapped around his body.

Rita pondered giving the sand back to the duende. Maybe he had a right to get mad, but she didn't know anything about them other than they were rude and mean—and perverted. Rita decided that a creature like that couldn't be reasoned with, and so she would have to confront it. No question. After all, the little shit had *pulled its pants down* in front of her. She shuddered as she remembered his minuscule penis.

Patricio gave Rita a long look. "So, has the duende been

---

[22] Looney bin

harassing you?"

Rita hadn't planned on telling her father the troubles, but he would find out eventually. She told him the story in between slurps.

"Well, at least the other students didn't see you. It was hard to miss so many goats with their funny haircuts or me in women's clothes." Patricio tweaked her nose. "Bueno, vámonos porque si no tu mama se va ha enojar.[23] You know how your mother gets when you come home late. We'll tell her I went to the hardware store to fix the pump, and that you had to check the math for me. You know those gringos will rip you off if you don't know their language."

"And if you know it," replied Rita.

Her father laughed and offered his arm like a gentleman to escort her to the truck.

WHEN THEY GOT HOME, Nana was busy praying to St. Jude. She had five candles lit, which was four more than usual, and this gave Rita the beginnings of a stomach ache.

-¿Vieja?-[24] called Patricio in a naughty child's voice. He was a brave man, but when it came to his wife's angry words, he was less than macho.

"She went to pray the Rosary," replied Nana.

"Woo hoo. Nos salvamos Rita!"[25]

Every other week Rita's mom would go to pray the Rosary with the barrio women. No doubt she would be telling the other women her woes, and soon all the children would find out about the duende. She would be the laughing stock of the school—again.

---

[23] Well, let's go, or else your mother will get mad.
[24] Old woman is a term of endearment.
[25] We saved ourselves, Rita.

Nana stopped praying and invited them to eat. She had made Rita's favorite, fried intestines and guacamole. She also made a big pot of beans. Nana gave Rita a significant look, -Y no los remoje como otras veces para que te den hartos pedos.-[26]

Rita rolled her eyes. She didn't care for beans much, but she didn't like to turn her Nana down. On most days, she would eat a small taco of dripping beans, but today, her Nana put a large cazuela in front of her with a teaspoon of mayonnaise. For more potency, Nana added onions on top.

Nana said grace in her usual fashion in Spanish, *Lord thank you for your many blessings. Let us always remember those who do not have enough to eat and give us the wisdom to take less, so they may have more. . . . And we also pray for Rita to beat the son of a bitch duende who's stalking her. . . . Amen.*

Rita and her father laughed until their sides hurt. Nana kicked them both under the table, admonishing them for disrespecting their guardian angels.

They told stories and ate, as was the usual custom. Nana told tales about her old boyfriends, and all the times her brothers and father chased them away with guns. Patricio told about his glory days when he picked cotton in the Cotton Belt and had stood up for black workers when the theater wouldn't let them sit in the seats below. Rita listened because she wasn't a very good storyteller, but she managed to talk about a kid who nearly electrocuted himself at the science fair. When the accident was over, his fingers were black, and his hair was standing on end. That was the only time someone else had been the focus of her peer's contempt, but her family didn't need to know that.

Rita admired her abuelita's gorgeous braid crown. She had

---

[26] And I didn't soak them ahead of time like I usually do, so they would give you the farts.

weaved in plastic flowers that looked real, and she wore one of her unusual white dresses with a blue shawl. Rita also noticed the light rouge on her cheeks and for the first time, Rita wondered if she didn't have a ghost lover or a real boyfriend. But that was impossible.

RITA WAS in her room reading another Sherlock Holmes mystery. Mama came home exhilarated from her prayer session. She poked in her head and gave Rita a prayer card and silver Rosary. Taking it gratefully, Rita put it on the nail with other scapulars and rosaries, above her head board. She kissed her mother and sat back with her dark thoughts. She couldn't focus because she feared what the duende would do to her once the sun went to its secret place.

That night, Rita was ready for a duende encounter. Even Bucho seemed confident. She wasn't going to lose this match. The crickets were chirping their miniscule but loud music. Some people hate the cricket serenade, but Rita enjoyed pretending that they were telling each other stories about their day. Maybe they were. After all, it was at night that the television was off and that the humans weren't making noise and disturbing everything. It was their quiet time.

Rita looked out the window and considered removing the onions and holy palm from her window. She stared out the window and caught a glimpse of a stray cat patrolling their yard. She managed to shift the onions around a bit but went to bed instead. She looked at her computer. She decided to research duendes. Maybe there were other ways to fight the creatures. She turned on her computer. The fan sounded like it was going out. *As usual.* The monitors blinked a funny orange, but she figured it had just glitched.

A faint smell began to emerge from the back of the monitor. It smelled like lemons. She looked behind it and noticed a small swirl of smoke coming out. Rita pulled the extension cord, and the monitor shocked her. The force pushed her back and slammed her head against the floor.

Water began to pool around her ears. She thought it was strange that she was crying so much. Bucho began to whine, but no one would come to her aid. Her parents were in the living room with Nana watching the newest Mexican soap opera, *Dos Amantes y Una Yegua,* and the sound was turned up high. Her analytical-self hoped they would smell the smoke or hear Bucho whine. The pain increased in her head and shot through her eyes, and the world vanished. Poof! Like a duende in summer time.

RITA WOKE UP the next day to her mother yelling at her to get ready. She was running 20 minutes late. Rita rubbed her eyes, and that stung more. There was sand all over her face and in her hair. She looked to Bucho. It was resting with a wreath of desert flowers around its neck.

"Rita! For the love of God. Look at your hair. There is dirt all over it. Brush it out and get ready for school. I don't want to know how it got there. Just get ready. Now!"

Rita quickly changed her clothes. She hadn't had time to slip into her nightgown. Last night was a blur. She saw her computer monitor, and it all came back to her. She grew furious. The monitor was burnt out. She remembered being hurt badly, but there was no blood on the floor. She looked to Bucho and noticed a note in the wreath. The paper was old and yellowed, with calligraphy writing in a font she had not seen in any library book.

It said, *Pansy sissy girl.*

Rita was beside herself. When the bus came, she stormed onto it without greeting the bus driver, Jimmy Shadow-Walker. He was a middle-aged Cocopah Indian who liked all the kids. Even the mean ones. He took one side glimpse at Rita and let her sit in the front seat.

Jimmy smiled at her from the mirror, and she smiled back weakly.

He said, "You know Rita. You're too small to be carrying the world's problems on your shoulders. All that does is mess up your back."

Rita laughed and stared out the window. The houses were so run down. Some of them had a bigger mess in the front than her Papi's junk yard. Others were immaculate with beautiful orange trees and cacti. But all of them were substandard in comparison to the mini-mansions owned by doctors and lawyers in the city.

She gazed over a ridiculous fluorescent orange trailer where none had ever been. There was a bright glow that followed the bus. She looked and rubbed her eyes. It appeared clear as the full moon in the desert night. The duende was floating along the bus, sitting with its legs crossed. She looked again and glanced at Jimmy to see if he noticed the glaring orange outfit. No one saw him except Rita. So, it seemed. When the bus stopped on County 14th, Jose's baby sister started pointing at it, but no one paid attention to her chubby fingers. They thought she saw another crop duster in the sky.

Jose sneered at Rita, as he made his way to the back with the cool kids. Rita looked at the duende, and it peered back at her. She waited for it to make an obscene gesture, but it occurred to her that she couldn't very well cut a fart in front of everyone. For certain, she couldn't open the bus window, as the windows were always stuck.

She looked back at the other kids.

"What are you looking at dog face?" said a random kid from the back of the bus.

That started a riot of barking and howling and Jimmy telling them to shut up, or he was pulling over. If they made the bus late, they would all get detention. That shut them up, but soon, a rain of stealth spit wads started. Rita was turned around, and one of the wads poked her eye. She started to cry, not from the pain but from the discomfort. There were still bits of sand from the morning.

Rita was so furious she bellowed out, "Chicken shit cowards! Pansy sissy assholes!"

Now Rita was a smart girl. She could also be a brave girl, but she had never retaliated or said any bad words. The children stopped for a brief moment. Jimmy even had a look of shock on his face, but he kept on driving. The spit wads started flying again. This distressed Rita. All she could do was hide behind the seat and crouch below the window. They were still getting her good, so she closed her eyes.

In the distance, she heard a faint buzzing from the back of the bus. It droned louder, forcing her to clamp her hands over her ears.

"You're spitting out bees!" yelled a high-pitched voice from the back of the bus.

"No, they're not bees! They're horse flies!"

The children began to scream. Jimmy stopped the bus with a jerking halt.

"Alright now! You kids better knock it off. There are no goddamn bees or horseflies anywhere!"

The boys and girls were still screaming in pain.

"That's it. You're all getting detention!" (Except for Rita who was sitting in front doing nothing but cowering.)

Rita looked out the window. The duende gave her a mean

glare, flipped her off, and floated towards the Mexican border.

When the bus got to school, it was thirty minutes late. Jimmy had radioed into the principal. The principal and the counselor were waiting at the curb.

Rita was excused from the fiasco, and even though the children urged the principal to let them see the nurse, they were each given a weeklong detention after school. Rita went to all her classes that day with an angry, tired, inability to sort out what had happened between the computer monitor to the bee incident. The duende had seemed to be helping her out, but he was still a jerk to her. It didn't make any sense at all, and she hated irrational behavior.

That day, school flew by at unusual speed. During lunch, a few of the students came up to talk to her to ask about the bus incident. She told them, and for once, she wasn't the brunt of the jokes. The other kids on the bus were.

"They're crazy!"

"Yeah, or they were on drugs."

"My history teacher told us about mass hysteria," said a girl with long brown braids. "Maybe it was like that."

Tina Saldívar piped in, "Maybe they're possessed."

This scared the conversation to an end. Tina smiled at Rita and went away.

Rita popped a fry into her mouth. Something was moving rapidly. She pulled it out and realized it was a humongous earthworm. They were squirming in her fry basket. Rita dropped them on the floor and spat out.

Mr. Levy came up to her. "Who the hell did that?"

"You *see* them?"

"See who? I'm talking about that healing gash on your head."

"What gash?"

83

Levy pointed the gash out without touching Rita's head. She ran her fingers where he pointed and encountered several spit wads. There was a large scab in the area where her hair was shorter. She hadn't noticed in her rush to get to school.

Levy had never known the Sifuentes to be abusive parents. In fact, they were the most attentive parents, given their tough work schedules. Besides, Nana was a great role model.

Rita looked at the confusion in Levy's face. "Well you see. I'm not much for going outdoors. I was looking at a bird's nest real close not long ago, and I fell out of the tree."

Levy looked at her disbelievingly. "You never told me that story; plus, that scab looks fresh."

"Yeah, well, I can have secrets." She paused for effect. "It is an *embarrassing* story."

"Oh please, *Ms. Sixteen* attitude. You once told me about the time the boys put boogers on your banana," retorted Levy.

"I don't tell you everything."

"Where did you get all that crap in your hair? You have mud and bugs in there. Go see the nurse. That wound could get infected."

Enrique, his partner, walked over just then with his usual jokes.

"Mija. Please, let me wash and cut your hair. I'll do it for free."

Rita stomped away to the girl's bathroom. She looked at herself in the mirror. Her face was streaked with dirt, and her hair looked disgusting. She was still furious.

"As if that damned faggot music teacher had a degree in beauty school. I don't know what Levy sees in him."

The toilet flushed, and she stopped short. *Had she said that out loud?* Out of the stall she could hear a resounding giggle.

A girl said in an exaggerated pitch, "Oh my gosh! Mr. Levy and Gill are a couple!" She went into another fit of giggles. The door opened.

Rita thought quickly. "That's not true. I was just angry!" She looked to see who the girl was and out walked her nemesis.

"You! You mean son of a bitch! You ruined my computer!" Rita lunged at it, but all she hit was the doorframe of a bathroom stall. For the second time that week, Rita was out cold.

THIS TIME, RITA WOKE UP in the emergency room.

The doctor was talking to her Nana in English.

"It's a minor concussion. What I'm worried about is that healing gash. That's five inches long. She should have gotten stitches. I had the nurse clean that out, but I would watch to see if she gets increased headaches or her vision gets blurry. Any sign that something's wrong. You bring her in or call. Here, take my card."

Her grandmother nodded respectfully.

Dr. Martin let Rita go home that day. Even if she had to stay longer, Rita would have lied about feeling better. The bill for the ride on the ambulance alone was $900. Nana was upset and wasn't sure where she was going to get the money for the expense. Amparo and Patricio could not afford anymore bills, and asking her friends for money was out of the question. Maybe she would trap herself a leprechaun. She knew they had money, but they were worse to deal with than the border patrol.

"How did you get here Nana?" She looked out and saw Mr. Levy and Mr. Gill.

Mr. Gill was pasty, and Levy looked ten years older.

"Hey come on. I'm not that bad off, am I?" They smiled the

fake smile of fast food restaurants worker and didn't elaborate.

On their way home, they didn't say much to her, except to ask if she was comfortable. Nana invited them into the living room. She wanted to offer them a late lunch as a thank you.

Nana went to the kitchen to get them some agua de arroz made of soaked blended rice. Rita brought out the best glasses and eyed the pair suspiciously.

"What gives?" asked Rita.

"Tell her." Levy nudged Enrique.

Enrique said, "No. You tell her. She's your favorite student. She's going to find out anyway."

Mr. Levy shook his head. "No, she just got out of the hospital."

"Ah fuck, just tell me!"

"Mouth, Rita, mouth." Levy went on to explain to Rita, checking to see her reaction, that Mr. Gill and he were not *just* roommates. They had been careful never to act like a couple in front of her. They were just two guys living in a conservative town trying to save money on the rent.

Rita looked at them and laughed. "I knew that! Man, you guys made it sound like there had been some kind of tragedy."

Mr. Levy paused and blushed. "Well, someone outed us at school."

"What?"

Levy searched her face. "You didn't say anything to anyone? Did you? We can't figure out how they found out. I mean—"

Rita looked at her feet. "Oh crap."

"Who did you tell?"

"You wouldn't believe me if I told you. Look, it doesn't matter how the school found out. I was ranting in the bathroom because I was angry at the comment you made about washing my

86

hair, and someone heard. I am so, so sorry!"

Mr. Gill looked confused. "One of the girls? But the a-hole who was telling everyone over the speaker was a man with a British accent. He sounded like the guy in that P.B.S. show, the fat lawyer."

"No. Look it's a long story. I'll deal with it—Wait, what are they going to do to you?"

"Well, they can't fire us because we'd sue. But you know how the students can get, and worse, the parents." Levy stared off into the distance. "We should just move somewhere where people will accept us."

Rita's eyes began to water. "No! Don't move. I'll be all alone in that school. I'm so sorry. I was just so mad with all the crap that's been going on."

"That's okay. Don't cry. We still love you." They reassured her. But the damage was done. Rita knew the students would have no mercy.

Nana came out to tell them the food was ready. For once, she felt comfortable enough to speak in English. "Who died?" This broke their tension as they walked into the kitchen.

Despite all the bad news, they managed to eat acceptable quantities of food in Nana's book, but it was hard not to eat. She had gone all out for the teachers. She made enchiladas in red sauce, rice, frijoles (a lot of frijoles), and arroz con leche for dessert. All the good smells wiped away their worries for a short time.

Sitting around the cramped table, they didn't tell Nana their bad news, but she proceeded to tell them Rita's trying news. At first, they thought Nana was telling a charra, but the punch line never came. They looked at Rita to see if Nana was missing a few screws, but Rita kept eating her enchiladas quietly.

Levy looked at Nana and Rita. "You're kidding me, right?

Enrique, what's this all about?"

"I don't know, Papi. I have seen some weird shit in my time. One time I could have sworn there was a woman looking inside my window. I was on the second floor of my tío's house. No one could have been out there so high, not even on a ladder. And there were no trees."

Nana answered expertly, "Bruja, maybe a vampire, but those are mostly a myth. Killed many times, just like the Aztecas. Gone."

"Hey, I can prove it! I mean it probably won't appear to you. Come into my room." She turned to her grandmother and asked, - ¿Nana pones un poquito de agua a hervir y échale dos cucharadas de aceite de oliva, por favor?-[27] Nana did as her granddaughter asked. Nana was making the base for the scrub Rita had been meaning to make for her teacher.

Rita brought them in to see her computer. "Look the duende was in here, and he blew out my monitor. I think he didn't mean to hurt me because I fell down and hit my head hard against the floor. Hence the gash. I think I could have died, but he fixed me up. That's why I have so much dirt in my hair. It was from the medicinal sand. It's magic sand. See?" They stared at the floor, but there was no blood stain.

Rita pointed to the computer. Indeed, the machine was burnt out. Nana walked in to tell her the water was boiling. "Put in a ¼ cup of the sand. It's right here. Rita pulled the jar from under her bed. It was halfway empty. "Well, just throw the rest in."

Here Nana went to the kitchen. Enrique inspected the computer. "Hey, I think the little shit put orange peels inside your computer."

Mr. Levy pulled out a tool from his pant pockets, a fancy one with a screwdriver and undid the back of the monitor. He took

---

[27] Nana, can you please boil a little bit of water and add two tablespoons of olive oil?

apart the other segments with expertise.

Sure enough, the computer was full of orange peels.

Levy looked at Enrique. "I don't think she can have that fixed. How did he get orange peels in there?"

"Magic." Answered Nana with the concoction in her hand.

Rita explained, "Just use a fingertip. No more. That should get rid of the rash."

Enrique accepted the jar and smiled at them kindly. He had been to three dermatologists, and no one had been able to cure his face. He put some on out of politeness and smiled.

Rita showed them her finger. "Look, yesterday I cut my finger. Today, there's not even a scar on it." They inspected it.

Levy pointed out her gash on the side of the head. "Rita! That's amazing. The gash is almost healed, and your hair has grown back. Though it's a funny color."

Rita inspected the grey dirty streak; it was almost silver, but not as glorious as her Nana's hair color. She bet the duende could have made it any color, but it looked the color of dry vomit. Even though she believed in the sand's properties, her mouth hung open. She pointed at his face.

"Holy shit." Mr. Levy ran a loving hand down his partner's face. "It's like a baby's butt."

Mr. Enriquez inspected his face and teared up. "I'm normal!"

Levy left the house committing himself to learn more about Mexican folklore and myths.

As they were driving away Rita yelled, "It's a facial scrub!" but to Mr. Enriquez, it was magic. They waved good-bye from their Subaru and rode off into the sunset leaving a cloud of dust.

Rita wanted to do more for them, but there was nothing else she could do. She knew they were not mad at her, but she was angry at herself. Rita could only do the honorable thing and get rid of the bastard that had been causing so much trouble. Before she went, she ate two more cups of beans and a large tomato. She grabbed a large plastic trash bag. If her attack failed, she would trap the duende and ship him to border patrol headquarters. They hadn't called their Nana after three years of waiting for her citizenship interview. That would teach them.

She walked out into the desert with Bucho by her side, but halfway there, she began to lose her nerve. Bucho walked a yard ahead of her and barked. It gave her courage. Rita looked at him and then at her destination.

She thought, *What if she failed? What if she couldn't trap him, and it just kept assaulting her like the kids with the spit wads?*

Rita looked around her for support. Bucho planted itself on the dirt and wouldn't budge until she followed. Rita looked to the sky. Another plane was making its rounds, except this one carried a large banner. It was probably some hokey marriage proposal from a gringo rancher.

She read the letters carefully.

Mr. Levy and Mr. Gill are fudge packers! The airplane looped around and on the other side it said,

Rita Sifuentes likes girls.

Rita was shocked. She didn't know what a lesbian was, but she knew she liked boys. That did it. She marched on with visions of how she would tackle the duende and sit on its face.

The desert was mute as always. The occasional breeze played with her messy hair. She reached the perimeter of the odd sand.

"Hey! Pendejo. Show yourself numb nuts!"

She stood there like an idiot yelling at the ground for a good ten minutes.

"Come out and show yourself, you midget!"

The sand swirled. She thought, *Maybe the duende didn't like being called short names.*

"Hey fairy fuck! Leprechaun lover! Come out and show yourself." She stomped her foot for emphasis.

The duende appeared behind Bucho and Rita and with one motion kicked them both in the rear—hard. Rita and Bucho turned simultaneously only to be kicked in the same fashion. This went on a couple more times until Bucho wised up and stood its ground.

The duende hovered over the sand. "Come get me chicken legs. Lanky sissy girl. Gusano marrano.[28] Girl lover."

"Fuck you, you dwarf dick!"

The duende turned purple. "Oh, isn't that educated. I'm sure we all must look the same to you. Come get me greaser girl. Wet back. Drug smuggler. You too, you, black ugly goat licker." The duende danced a funny jig and shook its butt at them. Slowly, it grabbed its pants and began to slide them down.

Rita and Bucho ran to the duende, and it vanished. Rita felt her world go topsy-turvy as she fell through an invisible door in the sand. She reached out for Bucho, but there was nothing she could do for her companion. They fell for what felt like an eternity and after a time, hit the ground. But they weren't killed, just hurt. She stood up shaking herself off and went to inspect Bucho. Miraculously, none of its legs were broken. It licked her hands whimpering.

"It's alright." She gave it a huge hug as it lapped the sand off her face.

She disengaged and went looking for the creature. They looked around, and the duende was nowhere in sight. The home which was more like a hole was plain. It had solid sand walls with

---

[28] An insulting rhyme that translates into worm-pig.

statues of sculpted tableaus. Tiny fingers waved hello from places Rita couldn't recognize. Some of them seemed to be dancing on the moon. Others rode on dolphin backs. One even sat in a lion's mouth. The duende was not wrong about one thing. They all looked the same to her; short and fat.

There was a tiny coffee table in the middle of the room. It was carved with beautiful intricate deep designs of flowers and birds. There was one tiny chair. It was white, weaved into a crazy web pattern, but it looked solid enough. There was no other furniture in the large space. She looked around for the duende, but he was absent. Bucho sniffed around, but he was at a loss for a scent.

"Let's explore."

They walked around from room to room. They were almost empty except for an occasional eggshell flower vase with unidentifiable plants and more statues of what she assumed were his friends and family.

"Wow, this place is really boring." Two hours later, Rita was *really* bored out of her mind. She was thirsty, even though the hole was cool. Bucho was also panting.

"Man, I wish I had a glass of water and a bowl for Bucho."

She gasped, as the objects materialized at her feet. She was hesitant to drink the water, but Bucho dove right in. She waited to see if anything would happen to it and felt like a cowardly homophobic jerk for doing so, but it seemed fine, so she drank hers.

Rita thought and said, "I wish I had $10,000." A small piece of trinket jewelry appeared before her. It was a tarnished silver amulet with an engraving of a lady with an ugly nose.

"I guess the wishes don't work at a large scale." She picked it up and put it in her pocket. "Payment for the computer, you short little bastard."

As if summoned, the duende appeared to her right and yanked her hair. It was naked. It looked like a three-year-old child, with lush white hair weaved into an intricate braid. Its body was smooth, a tan brown. Everything was minute and childlike, except for his wise face. And it might have been cute had the duende not stomped Rita's left foot.

"Ouch!"

The duende said, "Payback for stealing my sand, shitty spaghetti girl!"

Rita reacted quick as a rattle snake; she yanked its ear and slapped it around. The duende in turn wrapped its legs around her left leg and peed on her. Bucho tried to help by taking nips at it, but Rita was moving toward the wall. Rita slammed it hard and sat on it. She tried to fart, but nothing would come out. The duende pummeled her back, but she would not budge. She struggled so hard to flagellate her face was turning purple. With some effort, she farted so loud, it echoed throughout the room. Even Bucho whined in displeasure. The duende started making gagging and choking noises. It stopped. Rita got up to see how it was doing. It was prostrate on the floor. Its face turned a strange blue like the sea at sunset. She kicked it in the groin. The duende was still unresponsive. It looked like it was dying.

Maybe Rita had gone too far. Maybe she shouldn't have sat on it. She bent down to see if it was breathing. Rita poked it a few more times.

She gasped. "Oh crap. I think we killed the tiny fucker."

Suddenly, it opened his eyes and clamped down hard on her right hand with its infant mouth. The electric pain travelled all the way to her shoulder.

Rita waved it around as best she could, but it was heavy, heavier than its infantile body should have been. She ran against the wall, slamming it a second time, but the duende held fast.

"Get off me, you asshole. You're tearing my fingers off!"

Bucho charged the duende and grabbed it by the neck. Bucho pulled one way while Rita pulled another. He wouldn't let go. Rita fired another fart, and the duende released her. Bucho and Rita gave the duende such a beating, someone with a video camera for duende rights should have been recording the incident.

She said, running out of breath, "Do. You. Give Up?"

The duende spat at Rita in disdain. Bucho gave the duende a good shake.

"All right you ugly rotten alfalfa sprout." It wiped a wad of blood from its mouth. "You win."

Rita inspected the duende. She started to feel guilty. Its right eye was completely puffed up. A streak of blood ran down the corner of its mouth. There were marks and scratches all over the child-sized body. *Over what?* She thought, *A jar of sand and some nasty pranks?*

The duende saw the look in her eyes and was ready to give her more hell. Bucho squeezed, halting the creature's assault. Once it stilled, Bucho released the duende, and her pal spoke.

"Listen," said Bucho.

Rita and the duende looked at Bucho, awestruck.

"I have been watching you two fight for so long. I think what we have here is a cultural misunderstanding."

"Bucho! You can talk?" Rita was impressed by his vocabulary.

"Well," answered Bucho matter of fact, "I made my wish in the cave, as well as you. My other wish is that you two just be happy. There's no point in fighting. Let me tell you my story."

"This is bound to be a winner," muttered the abused duende.

"I used to fight with the white goose all the time. His brothers would gang up on me, and I, in turn, would bite their tails when they were not expecting it.

"One day, one of the geese asked us why we were fighting when there was so much land. After all, I had my drinking bowl, and they had their drinking bucket. We could take turns sleeping on the back of the house or under the shade of the tree. So, from then on, the geese stay under the trees in the morning, and I go swimming in the pond and vice versa. We just had to come to an agreement and accept our differences.

"You two have been fighting over an insignificant jar of sand. And you, Mr. Duende—"

"Please, call me Charlie." It spat blood on the pristine floor.

"Charlie, don't you have anything better to do than to harass my mistress over a trifle? You clearly have more sand than you need. This home gives you all you desire and more. It seems to me that you suffer from boredom, maybe even loneliness."

"Yeah, loser," said Rita, remembering what he had done to her teachers.

"Tut tut," continued Bucho, "you have no room to talk. For years I have been watching you with some consternation as you sit at your bright block doing this or that. But you never go out and play with friends. If I could make friends with the geese, I think you can make a few friends as well."

Rita looked at Charlie.

"Look," said Bucho, "just apologize to one another and call a truce. Better yet, become friends."

"Well," said Rita, "friends might take a while after all the fucked-up things you did."

"What?" replied the duende. "You nearly killed me with your wretched stench!"

"So did you with your evil prank! And you outed Mr. Levy and his boyfriend! That is unforgivable."

"Well you called me a fairy fuck. I hate fairies! They are the worst!"

Bucho barked and growled. The wish had worn off, but the meaning was clear. Rita and Charlie held a staring contest for a few intense minutes.

Rita softened her look. She averted her eyes and looked at the mess they had created in its once neat home. The statues were askew, some crushed. The table was dinged on the corner. She thought about what Bucho said. *Was she the reason she didn't have friends? Did she build a wall that kept them out?* After all, she had no problem talking to the group after the bus incident, and she had liked some of them. Maybe, she had been part of the problem.

She breathed out and gave Charlie a side-glance. "Well, I'm willing to call a truce, Charlie. I promise I won't take any of your sand and will do my best to keep strangers away from your home, if you promise to stop being such a nasty short—"

Bucho growled and pawed at Rita's leg.

"Okay, peace?" asked Rita.

"Peace but don't keep strangers away," Charlie mumbled. "In fact, send some of those mean children over . . . if you want."

"Are you going to be alright?"

"Well," said the duende, "I could use a little help." Rita wished for a medicine kit and fixed Charlie as best she could along with her scratches. She was sure it could patch itself up magically, but she felt she owed it.

She thought to herself, *I've been cruel to it—to him.*

She cared for him as Nana would for her and discovered his ears were ticklish. She even went so far as to comb and braid his luscious hair, which seemed to please the duende very much, but not in a perverted way. Bucho was the only one who was not hurt. He looked at them, wagging his tail.

When Charlie let them out of the hole, along the far wall, an elevator appeared where none had been before.

"Come back and visit," said Charlie. "But please, don't fart in my house. You stinky pedorra."[29]

Rita smiled and waved good-bye, and Bucho barked happily.

When they got home, Rita's mother and father were waiting anxiously.

"What happened?" asked her father giving her a tremendous hug.

Her mother chastised her for the condition she was in.

"I won, sort of. We called a truce."

Nana walked outside and asked, -¿Que es un *truce*?-

Rita explained that it meant peace, and her Nana crossed herself.

- ¡Imposible!- she said.

Patricio explained again in Spanish, and Nana was shocked. In all her life, she had never heard of someone making a truce with a duende. Times *were* changing. Duendes were not what they used to be when she was a girl.

- ¡Que lastima!-[30] she exclaimed.

Rita took a long shower, even though she was very good about conserving water. She put on a cool housedress her mama had made for her, a yellow one with embroidered blue flowers. Her hair was softer than it had ever been, and it managed to stay in one place. When she walked into her room, she was surprised to find the orange smell had disappeared. Her room looked brighter than usual, permeated by the scent of Saguaro flowers. There was an

---

[29] This translates into a female farter.
[30] What a shame!

inked note on her computer screen:

I can only fix so much with magic. Reputations are a different matter, and I can't control the fucked-up things humans do. Levy and Gill will have to deal with that mess.

- Charlie. P. S. Don't forget to check your pocket.

Rita pulled the old pendant from her messy pant pocket. She showed it to her mother.

"Hmm, this is very old. We should try to sell it."

THE FOLLOWING EVENING, when everyone had heard the story about Rita vs Charlie enough times, Patricio drove the family to the antique dealer in town. He was an old dried up man from Mississippi. He was a stingy old man who didn't like anyone without a full billfold.

"What do you want?" he asked gruffly when the family of Mexicans walked in.

Rita stepped up. "We have something we would like you to price for us."

The old man snorted in contempt. "Well quit wasting my time. Let's see what you got."

Rita handed over the pendant. The old man scrutinized it while Nana noted his facial expressions and the new twinkle in his eyes.

He said, "It's a piece of garbage, but I'll give you $15, $20 tops."

Before Rita could answer, Nana grabbed the pendant away from the old man and farted in his direction. She said, -Vámonos.

Este pinche viejo tacaño nos quiere ver la cara.-[31]

They left and went to another antique dealer. This dealer was a younger woman in her thirties. She was not unfair and was friendly to everyone who walked into her store.

"Let's see here." She pulled out a book from her shelf and read carefully. "Wow! Where did you get this?"

She looked to all their faces.

"I found it in the desert."

"What a find! Not unusual being in the Southwest. A lot of hacenderos from rich Mexican families wore these pendants. Usually a matriarch. This one is not in such good shape, and I will be honest, I don't have the money or the market for this. I'll deal in coins. But, I would say this piece is worth $5,000. You might have to get it cleaned, although some collectors might fancy the story of a pretty girl finding the piece in the desert."

Rita blushed. Nana gasped and put her hand over her heart. For once, Amparo cut loose in her joy and let out a shout. Patricio couldn't speak.

"We could fix the water pump!" said her Rita.

Her mother added, "I could get a new sewing machine."

The dealer gave them the information of a friend of hers in California. Within the month, the piece was sold for $6,000.

Indeed, the pump was fixed, and Rita's hospital bills were taken care of, *mostly*. Amparo bought a new sewing machine and started making multi-purpose dresses on the side. In time, she started doing that full time, which made her a happier person. Nana got some new dentures from Mexico, which she had denied she needed for several years. Even Bucho got a foot-long rawhide bone for his bravery and a trendy cloth water bowl that Rita could carry and fill in the desert. After the money was spent, there was

---

[31] Let's go. This old tight ass wants to rip us off.

not enough money for a new computer. Rita didn't need one. Rita suspected Charlie had put new components in her beat-up old thing. Instead, Patricio put $700 in the bank, which was more money than they had ever had and took the family out to Red Lobster.

Mr. Levy and Mr. Gill did not move away from Silver, after all, but they had to deal with harassing phone calls and graffiti on their car. Eventually, they began talking to the school about sexuality and to the parent's shock, homosexuals. Some people still called them names and made jokes about them, but they kept it to themselves. They never accepted the pair like bigots are wont to do.

Rita and Bucho became great friends with Charlie. She even made a few more friends in the science club. While hanging with the neighborhood kids, she discovered that she had a good pitching arm. No one in the barrio could hit her fastball. She would try out for softball next year.

And Charlie. Well, when all was said and done, he had the best year of romping and playing tricks in decades. He even managed to make friends with a fat fairy in the canal next to his hole. One, who was not unbearable and nasty.

Not all problems were resolved. The family still struggled, and Patricio still worked like a dog. For a short while, everyone was content and happy.

Never Really Alone

Isella Jones read his last text message with disgust—*See ya tomorrow night, hottie.* She glared at the flame emoji. She replied—*No. 2 busy prepping for X-mas dinner. Plus, I got one more day of school & A-team meeting. Gotta go. -xo cRymson.* She glared at the phone as she nibbled at a stubborn cuticle on her middle right finger. Isella and Richard Portia had been going steady since junior high, over five years ago. He had always been a sappy romantic, but ever since he went to college last year, to M.I.T. no less, he was changing, and although she expected some change, she wondered if it was time for her to end things.

"Ouch!" The cuticle stung, as she ran her fingers through her curly hair that reminded her of abandoned rope coils in junkyards. She began to write down the pros and cons about their relationship and put her pencil down.

She got up and looked out the widow to see if her mom had come home, and all she was greeted by was a row of sterile houses, the thick brick wall, and beyond that, the endless desert outside Aspire. Aspire was a newly established, gated community outside of Yuma, AZ. Everybody wanted to live there. She, on the other hand, wanted to get as far away as possible to a college in the east coast. That familiar pang of guilt made her sit at her desk with the weight of the world on her shoulders. Isella analyzed the last trinket he sent her via mail, a sun catcher with red and orange flowers, made out of thick floss.

As far as she could remember, Isella had always been the level-headed one. He had asked her out twenty times, once in front of his nerdy debate friends, and she had turned him down gently every time. She started going out with him when he brought her a bouquet of hand-picked flowers for Valentine's Day, common wild yellow daisies like the ones growing on the side of watered citrus fields. By that point, Rich was taller and more muscular. That day, something about the way he slouched and wore his ripped jeans swayed her, or maybe, she had daddy issues like every other dummy in school.

Now, she tore up the blank paper, sticking her nose back into her physics book. The formulas and examples were a haze as she mulled over why they were still dating each other. She sat at her sparse wooden desk and looked over at the Christmas gift for him. It was in an enormous box, embraced by shiny red paper and crowned with a large silver bow. Isella had put the most considerate present ever in that box along with some expensive hard cover books by the author they both liked, Inia Beginnings, the top-ranking mystery writer of her time. She had spent hours crafting his gift and knew he would love it, at least pre-hottie boyfriend would have. He also knew all the books she read and made it a point to buy him two hard cover books she hadn't read yet. Even M.I.T. boyfriend would appreciate that touch.

"What are you doing, studying so hard and driving yourself crazy?" she asked, swiping at her annoying long curls that poked her left eye. "No one's giving tests or quizzes tomorrow." The clock on her phone read 8:30 p.m. on the dot. Against better judgement, she logged onto her gaming system, the latest Kanji. It was a rare gift her estranged father got her over the summer.

The Kanji, unlike other gaming controllers, nested in her right hand. It was a comfortable glove with buttons housed in the palm of her hand, and the trigger attached to the index finger. The controller was supposed to prevent carpel tunnel, but mostly, it looked cool with its silver encasing and colored lines tracing bones with phosphorescent lines. She chose a steel blue for her decorations and made her irresponsible father pay through the nose.

She was a fanatic of *Escape the Horde*, a combination zombie shooter game with puzzles and locks. Isella preferred the mental challenges to the undead killing sprees and was proud of her records for cracking each puzzle and opening each lock. She ranked number seven out of all the players in the U.S. and 21 globally. Analyzing the list, she vowed to demolish what were surely Japanese third graders that skewed the rankings. Regardless of player nationality, Isella was often criticized for being a camper by other gamers, but she preferred to snipe zombies from a distance rather than meet them head on. Most kids would complain that she wouldn't help or cure them, but she ignored their whining and kept on surviving one sharp shoot at a time. Moving from clue to clue like a Latina Sherlock Holmes with a sniper rifle and shotgun.

She was on level 4 when her friend Viddie, chatted, "Hey, The Boy come over yet?"

Isella took her sniper rifle and took out a few more zombies before she put on her headset. She made sure first that The Boy, Annihilator69, was not logged in, just in case he could do so from the airplane. That would be absurd, but she had never been on a plane and remembered 1StupidSamurai had bragged about playing on a flight.

"He's flying in tonight. His mom's picking him up. I don't think I'll see him until after Christmas. Mom has me making all the dinner preparations because she has a double."

"That blows, but girl, you ready to give him the *best* gift of all? I mean, he's been waiting a long, long time to unwrap *that* gift."

In light of her doubts, she paused thinking over her response. Most couples would have done it by now, heck some after a few days, but Isella always imagined the worst-case scenario, and the worst-case scenario was her being stuck in a trailer with a neglected daughter.

"Hey, don't stop talking about *that present*. I'm all ears," said a strange, older boy.

She hesitated in case it might be Rich, but it wasn't. "Screw you," spat Isella, muting him out with two clicks of her index finger. She huffed. "Let's go to a private room." She created a room just for her and Viddie and called it "Piss Off Pervy Weirdos". Isella started a new match.

"I'm not ready," she said.

Viddie's exasperated sigh could be heard throughout the digital zombie realm. "You want to stay a virgin forever?"

"I'm 17, stupid-pendeja." Isella missed her shot as she aimed for a speedy ghoul. "Damn."

This one was a runner with a jaw flapping in the breeze, a crap spotted yellow t-shirt, and wrecked white jeans highlighting the gore and pain. She clenched her jaw, aimed again, and blew its head clean off, just as its fingers neared the back of Viddie's avatar.

On the screen, Viddie was wearing the head of a lion and silver armor and successfully guiding a horde of 20 plus undead towards some traps she had crafted. Her partner was better at running and killing masses than being stealthy, so Isella always had to help her crack puzzles. Still, they were a great duo and often played against other teams. Isella *mmmed* in appreciation as the horde plummeted into a hole and caught on fire. As Viddie did a virtual arm pump of victory, she left herself unguarded, as another swift zombie emerged from behind a dumpster. It was about to jump on Viddie, when Isella dispatched it with a quick head shot.

"I got you girlfriend."

"Isella—"

"Dude, don't use my name!" She hated when Viddie used her real name, which happened too often. CrYmsonSavage was what she preferred.

"CrYmson," she said. "Savage, nobody cares if you're a virgin anymore. Come on, even your mom put you on the pill."

"Why do you keep bringing that up?" Isella launched a grenade at another large group of ghouls.

"I'm scared!" said Viddie in a mock voice as she sliced through other assailants. It was her gamer tag line that she plagiarized from YouTube, but Isella wondered if Viddie truly was scared.

"I beg to differ," said the same strange voice, which cracked at the r. Standing right next to her muscular form on the secluded rooftop was a regular looking player in an army outfit. He didn't have a fancy skin or any upgraded weapons—"He" stood there smiling with his blonde hair and sparkling green eyes. The sole upgraded feature on his avatar. The eyes shimmered left to right, and under other circumstances, she would have thought they were cool, but there was something menacing about them.

"What!" she cried. "This is a private room! How did you get in here?"

He did a stupid dance that ended in an inhuman series of flips touching his right pinky to left foot, right before he landed.

"I got my ways. Gorgeous."

His voice was thick, and she couldn't tell if he was 16 or 26, but the cracks in the speech were not unusual for younger Freshman. It was the same voice from before, which had sounded older. *Or was he messing with her?* Isella deleted the room and called her friend.

The phone rang once, and Viddie picked up.

Isella asked exasperated, "What was that? How did he get in?"

"He's a piece of trash hacker. I reported him as you were rage-deleting our awesome room," answered Viddie who knew her friend Isella was crazy paranoid of meeting pedophiles and other weirdos online. Isella played to talk to Rich every day, but these days, she and Viddie had spent more time on the game with Viddie always being Rich's secret cheerleader in this relationship. In Viddie's estimation, what Isella and Rich had was practically marriage. Plus, Viddie had lost her virginity on a double dare two months before to some third-rate football player on another friend's couch. Even though she would never admit it, Lizzie knew her bestie regretted it. To make matters worse, Isella had driven her to the free clinic to get tested for H.I.V., and once the joyful results came back, they never spoke of the incident again.

"It was too weird, Vid I've never heard of anyone doing that before. It was creepy . . . and gross." She shuddered as she imagined an obese nasty man with a dirty beard playing online. Food plastered on his gamer t-shirt too tight for his paunch and acid jeans too retro for today's fashion. Viddie laughed her high-pitched squeaky laugh that made even CrYmsonSavage cringe. It was the same giggle she let escape when she got the negative test results.

"Well, good night," she said curtly. "Wish me luck for tomorrow."

"What's going on tomorrow?" ask Viddie chewing on something crunchy.

"I have to go food shopping. Weren't you listening? The meat's on sale at Don Julio's, and Mom will be too busy at the hospital to go to the store. Might as well let me do everything, but she's doing all the fun Christmas shopping."

Viddie snorted. "Girl, on your Mom's budget, she'll be hitting the thrift store."

They both laughed because it was true. Ever since her father left them when she was just ten, her mother was always working double shifts at the hospital. She worked hard so that Isella could be well-provided for and focus on school. Her mother was a registered nurse in the cardiology department, but the Sperm Donor, as they both called him, had left them with a sizeable house and the mortgage to go with it. Often, Isella would plead for them to move from that fancy neighborhood with perfect lawns and intricate holiday decorations they couldn't compete with. But her mother loved that house. Even though they made it paycheck to paycheck, Isella hated how her mother struggled, so she managed to contribute by selling unique collectibles and hand-crafted goods online. Sometimes if she was bold enough, she would sell merchandise at the swap meet along with elderly couples and vendors from California. That was a great deal of sweaty work and talking, which she hated. eBay was the way to go.

Her top seller that week had been a dime from the 1800's with a woman sporting a large bust. She wasn't sure if it was worth thousands of dollars because she had started dabbling with coins and hadn't done enough research. In the end, she sold it for $200. She had bought it at a yard sale for $10 from a kind old lady who no longer cared about material goods. Isella would have paid more for it, but all she had were ten dollars. That ugly coin would let Isella and her mom afford the groceries and leave a little extra for some lipsticks for her mom's Christmas gift.

She went through her nighttime routine, careful to floss every tooth and brush each quadrant, 26 times. She lined up five skin-care bottles ranging from a cleanser to scrub. As a registered nurse, her mom had cut a deal with the hospital's dermatologist, and she got free samples, rather large samples. Isella suspected her mother was sweet on that doctor, but she never pried.

She inspected herself in the mirror. She had one zit, one lousy zit, on her right cheekbone, but otherwise, her creamy light skin was the envy of most girls. Her soft reddish-brown hair, a genetic contribution from her loser father, was *not* the envy of anyone. Her curls had a mind of their own. Sometimes protruding at odd angles no matter how many times she sprayed or pulled them back. The one saving grace was that waist-long hair was in style, even rebellious messes. When it was wet, the burden went past her buttocks, and she often fantasized about cutting it short. Her perfect arched eyebrows, which her mother had taught her to pluck to save money, looked professional. Her large round hazel eyes, an angled nose, small for her face, made most people think she was pretty, but her avatar worthy full lips are what boys and some girls admired. The one feature that vexed her was that she was small all-around, except for her breasts. She was a damned living Barbie doll, to underclass boys that decided they were boob experts and let her know daily now that Rich was away at college. She wanted normal A-cup breasts, proportional to her frame. The lack of ratio made it almost impossible for her to find clothes that fit, so Isella would often have garments altered, which was not cheap, not even at barrio rates from her mom's old neighborhood, a secluded Mexican neighborhood without walls or guards at the front. Her mother's godmother, Doña Luisa, hemmed her pants for $5 and other alterations for less, but she lived far away from Aspire, as poor people were meant to live.

Isella went to bed and stared at her game console which she forgot to turn off. The green light beckoned her to start one more match. Out of curiosity, she turned on the T.V. and saw she had a new friend request, "Friendster17". It was him—the piece of scum hacker. In her message in-box was a pathetic video he sent with a face of a teddy bear covering the lens, not his real face. *Coward,* she thought to herself.

"Sorry, if I scared you. I just want us to be friends." He made the bear look pathetic by lowering its head, so she could see some details of his messy room. He was no doubt a boy judging by the piles of clothes and large mismatched sneakers in the background.

He continued, "I mean when you play. Not in real life. That would be weird. I'm not looking to sniff your cyber panties or anything, but you can't blame me for thinking you are gorgeous. That's a fact. You're as pretty as the Virgin Mary." His voice cracked on the r, again.

Isella froze. She had no real picture of herself anywhere in public, especially online, but CrYmsonSavage was pretty attractive, crafted with long black hair and well-proportioned body parts, including the chest. Still, she turned off the console and T.V. and vowed not to play until after Christmas when she could report him. Unlike other gaming companies, this one took bullying and stalking seriously, but still, she worried. Even so, she filled out the form, detailing what had happened. For emphasis, she checked the "sexually inappropriate with minors" option. That would raise some red flags.

Imagining that things would get worse with Friendster17 or that her man in real life would push her to do something she simply was not ready to do, Isella fell asleep into a restless slumber. She shivered as images of unsupervised sofas pierced her head, her new cyber-stalker looking through the expansive window as Rich took advantage of her.

THAT NIGHT, SHE DREAMT a fat man with a long beard was playing on her Kanji. He was chatting with random players, even some in Japanese, pecking at letters with her gaming glove, and doing a great job of killing zombies. He ended the round with a tough puzzle. He was supposed to open a lock on a safe, to find another clue, to get to the next level. She hadn't played this round, but she was sure the numbers to the lock were on the map, either as street signs or numbers on the buildings.

The man whistled and said, "I remember a 7 from the first house bedroom poster, 4 from the gas station name, 28 graves in the cemetery, and what else, Mirthful Mistletoe?"

"Count the buildings," said Isella enjoying this dream.

He turned around startled. "Oh, Candy Cane Curls! What are you doing awake?"

"What are doing in my room, Fat Glitter Bomb?" she asked taking in his unusual clothing and trying to match his quirky word play. He turned a deep red, but he smiled and counted the buildings slowly.

"Fair point, Candy Cane Curls. I'll get to that," he answered trying a series of combinations.

"Go in order of the numbers," she advised and added, "Purple Paunch Patrol".

He punched in 4, 7, 10, 28, and the lock opened.

She smiled. "Nice." He stood up, and she analyzed his full form. He did have a cute paunch, but what struck her was the long white beard and hair, a foot past his neck. Both were neatly groomed, and she held back an urge to run her fingers through both. He looked very much like a medium-sized Santa, except he had no glasses or moustache. His suit was also not red, but purple with patterned glitter in the shapes of aberrant swirls and stars.

It was lovely.

He gave her a sad look. "You're probably wondering what I'm doing here, Dreamless Dearie."

Isella giggled. "Playing on my Kanji, obviously, Glittery Goofball. This dream is *so* weird.

"Are you Santa Clause? Or a shameful distant relative."

She waited and added, "Are you a gay relative?"

It was his turn to chuckle. "No, better, Sassy 'Sella."

"Oh, come on!" She snorted. "That was a cheap try."

"I protect you. Have been for years."

Isella moved to get off her bed, starting to get annoyed, and stepped on the thick carpet. A sharp pain made her gasp. "Ouch!" She stepped on a pin from an old sewing project she attempted some months ago. She recognized it because it was a red-butterfly pin, and she now used blue pins with smaller round heads. Isella massaged her foot. When she looked up, the Purple Pest was gone.

"What?" she asked no one as a drop of blood pooled on her toe. She looked around, under the bed. In her closet. The bedroom door was locked, and she was about to go search the house, when she began to grow drowsy. She tried staying awake, but her head clouded. Before long, she was curled up in her bed above the covers, as her impatient avatar stood waiting for her to start the next battle.

THE NEXT MORNING, Isella was sullen. She sat at the kitchen table. Her mother was in a rush. This time, she wore her Minion scrubs, which Isella had bought her as a joke. Of course, her mother loved to wear them. Today, her hair was slicked back with a Monarch butterfly pin in her hair. She would be working with children.

"What's the matter, hon?"

Isella looked at her dark coffee and circled her right finger along the rim of the cup. "Mom." She paused unsure how to frame the next questions. "Does dementia or schizophrenia run in our family . . . or his family?"

Mom gave her a concerned look and laughed. "No sweetie. Why?"

She looked at the older image of herself, her stressed-out mother. They had a similar frame, petite—cursed with expansive breasts. Her skin was tan, unlike Isella's light skin. The major difference was her mother had a large indigenous nose and long thick black hair. Isella so wished she had those thick locks and not the mop mess from the Sperm Donor. She noticed new wrinkles at the sides of her mother's eyes and some forming around her warm smile. Isella grinned. "Oh, no reason. I was just studying psychology, and it made me think."

Her mother gave her a pensive look, a quick peck on the cheek, and rushed out the door. "I left the full list on the refrigerator! Text me if you have questions."

Of course, Isella had no questions. She was a better cook than her mom, and had a knack for bargaining, even at Anglo grocery stores. Isella held the list and noted the confectionary sugar.

"Somebody's making wedding cakes or buñuelos." Those were their favorite pastries, and they only made them on holidays or special occasions. The wedding cakes were small baked balls of buttery dough suffocated in powdered sugar, a hit for any potluck or party, but the prospects of this indulgence weren't enough to erase the memory of the strange fat man in the purple suit or that idiot hacker, Friendster Fool. She thought hard and checked her phone. Rich hadn't sent her a text or called.

It was 5:45 a.m., and she needed to head for school for a 6:30 a.m. meet-up. She was tired and wanted to call in sick, but like her boyfriend had done, she wanted to get into early college admissions and that meant joining clubs. That meant being on the A-team for Academic Decathlon, and fortunately, she was the top player and unofficial team captain, which was a great honor for a Junior. She was in other clubs, but this one always met at 6:30 a.m. and later in the evenings to accommodate the Mormons going through Seminary,

112

which was three quarters of the team. She always joked that instead of preparing to be missionaries, they were preparing for a hard-married life of lack of sleep and large households.

She slid into the large truck and warmed up the car for five minutes appreciating the glorious sunrise. The transition from pink to a passionate orange was magic. It hadn't rained in the desert for a while, and there was little green. In the distance, a whippoorwill arced gracefully in the sky. Then it swooped down and caught something, small and furry. Isella wanted to be the majestic bird, but often, she was the rodent. She put her foot to the pedal one more time, said a prayer to the universe, and drove off.

On schedule, Viddie texted her. Isella ignored it because she needed to go over the pointless facts for the morning session. That year, the teams were studying early American history, and she wanted to wow her coach with her knowledge on pioneer women. She had read *Filaree,* a sad story about a pioneer woman and also read about women who dressed like soldiers to fight in the Civil War. The study had been fascinating, making the rote memorization of regular history almost fun.

Isella looked at the rows of lettuce on her right, as workers stooped and rose in a repetitive motion. She would be in school in 15 minutes, making her 30 minutes early. The familiar chime made her lose focus off the road. She glanced at the text. *Busy?* She was about to respond, when her car began to lurch, as she was turning off 18th Street to reach the school. She slowed. Cars honked. She cursed back. She steadied the steering wheel and pulled over to the side of the road, away from some parked cars, before the front of the car dipped unnaturally, making her scream. Isella breathed like her coach had taught her to do before a test.

She got out of the pick-up, to inspect the fender, certain she hadn't hit anything. Sure enough, the front tire had languished in sad defeat. She looked at the back of the truck. There was a lovely spare tire, and no jack. Isella stood on the side of the road, hoping some angel would stop, but most drivers were focused on getting to work in the morning. Staring at her phone, she debated whether she should call him or her mom or walk to school or hitch a ride. Rich was far from school, and her mom wouldn't pick up while doing rounds. It would take her twenty minutes or so to get school on foot if she jogged, which she would do because Isella hated missing meetings or being late.

She looked back one last time as a majestic Dodge Demon whizzed past her. Isella headed for her school, when a small dark car stopped behind her. The sun wasn't fully up, and the headlights were bright, so she couldn't make the model or the year. She trained her eyes on the driver. He was tall and skinny. As he approached, she recognized Harry Arlott, a shy member of the C team.

"Hey," he said raising his hand and dropping it as quickly.

"Uh, hi," she said. "Harry, right?"

He guffawed staring at his feet. "Yeah."

That is why she never talked to him. He couldn't sustain a conversation with her without him clamping down or laughing like an idiot.

"I got a flat," she said.

"Well, I can change it now, or if you want, I can do it after the meeting. I'm sure Mr. Harris won't mind if we're late for first period if we talk to him." He smiled.

"Hmm," she said, as she thought about her options. "Actually, yeah. Let's do that. I hate being late for school. Plus, I have no jack." She grabbed her backpack, took a piece of paper, and wrote *Going to get a jack. Don't tow my car, assholes* and put it on the dashboard window. She thought better of it and added the same message in Spanish.

Harry made a regal motion with his arm circling it like he had seen it in a B.B.C. special and urged her to the car as he opened the door for her.

What a weirdo, she thought, but smiled against her better judgement. Isella was impressed by the cleanliness of the compact car. The interior was made of smooth black leather, and she cringed to think how expensive that stereo had been. She fluttered her fingers over the intriguing cassettes he had organized in a clear plastic box in the console between the seats.

He sat awkwardly. "Sound is better than plugging your phone in. Do you like The Cure?"

"Sure," she said, but she knew little about the band other than her mother wanted to marry Robert Smith, which was gross. His hair was disgusting, and he looked like a middle-aged mime with all the white caking on his face

"My favorite track is 'Just Like Heaven'," he said and explained the sequence of albums, which made the ride go by fast. His voice wasn't unpleasant and despite his useless information, there was something humble about the way he talked.

"So, which is your favorite?" he asked.

Isella answered without thinking, "Love Song," which was a total lie, but that had been the song her parents had danced to at their trailer trash wedding, and her mother sang it often, when she was depressed.

"Classic," he said. "Are you going to the dance next month?"

Isella flushed and turned towards him. "Nope. I hate dances."

Harry shook his head slowly. "Nah, they're not so bad. I'm taking my little sister this year. She's a Freshman."

"Why? She can't find her own date?" *And is she an awkward mess like you?* she thought.

"No. Quite the opposite. She has a social media following like you would not believe, and in real life, the boys are chasing her constantly. Because she is, well, a vixen with an attitude which makes her more desirable. It's Jell-O Girl, but don't tell anyone."

"Jell-O Girl is your sister?" There were few Instagram accounts that Isella followed. But Jell-O Girl—who like her never posted pictures of herself—was her feminist hero.

"She *is* really beautiful, and I don't mean that in a weird pervert way," he explained. "But she doesn't want a boyfriend—or girlfriend for that matter. Can't be a hater."

Isella laughed in earnest. "Yeah, can't be."

"If you saw her, you'd understand," he said drumming to the final beats of the song, "so I've sadly been appointed to be her lord panty protector."

Isella laughed out loud. "Purple Protector would be P, P, P Proud."

He gave her a quizzical look. "Who?"

They got out of the car into the near-empty student parking lot and for a moment he stopped awkwardly. Isella was sure he was going to keep inquiring about the Purple Protector or about the dance, but instead, he made another flamboyant gesture and urged her forward.

Isella inspected his feet and realized he was wearing different shoe; one red Converse and a silver one. He also wore mismatched socks, red and silver on opposite feet. Harry lifted up his pants. "It's laundry day."

She laughed again for a time, and she tried to quiet down, as they walked into the classroom together. When they entered, Coach Ellis, an enthusiastic history teacher was going over Native American history. They were token facts, nothing in-depth.

"Well, well, glad you could join us," she said with a grimace that highlighted the teeth she rarely flossed. Isella suspected her parent had been economically challenged, too, and didn't teach her any proper dental hygiene.

"Sorry coach," she said without repentance. "I got a flat tire, almost died. Immediately afterwards, I was saved by this knight in shining armor."

The girls in the class *ooohed*, which made her smirk.

"My knight with one silver shoe, sans sword."

He was not to be outdone. "With pleasure, my lady!" He made a delicate arc with his left arm and bowed. The other team members snickered.

"Oh my God!" said Jerry from the B-team. "He does have a silver shoe! Just one!"

"Okay, okay," said Coach Ellis trying not to laugh and keep class decorum, "be serious!" She slammed her empty coffee cup on the desk and went on lecturing as the rest of the group grew disciplined.

Isella took out her green binder with all her notes. The sections were organized with tabs and Post-its. Each color was a specific subject. All of her coaches admired her work often telling the team members to follow suit. She also took out her refurbished laptop and took notes out of politeness because she had already memorized everything. She stole one more glance at Harry, and he winked back at her.

CONVINCING COACH HARRIS their science coach who also happened to be their first period physics teacher had not been so difficult. Besides, it was a review day, and she and Harry were both getting an A in the class.

On their way back to the truck, Isella chose a random cassette. "Is this any good?"

Harry popped it in. "The Cars. Rule."

He smiled at her, as a sappy love song started to play.

"Bleh," she said, "why do you listen to this stuff?"

He shrugged his shoulders and sang to the next song. As he neared the spot where the truck should have been, he answered, "It reminds me of my mother."

Isella sat in the car, a boba[32] in a bad comedy, her mouth wide open. "Where the hell is my truck?"

Harry got out and came back in. "Looks like it was towed."

"What?" She ran her hands through her hair, tangling the right finger. "Where could it be?" She saw other cars parked there, and she followed Harry.

Her truck had been by a lettuce field, and she trudged over to one of the workers harvesting each lettuce head with precision.

"Hey," she started in English until the woman with the large scarf gave her a befuddled look. -Aquí estaba mi troca.-[33] Isella pointed at where her truck had been.

The tired woman nodded and explained that the foreman called for a company to tow it. Isella asked a few more questions.

She got into his car slamming the door. "The foreman called a towing company but not the cops."

Harry smiled at her. "Do you think that lady needs water?" Before she could answer, he grabbed a bottle of water, stepped out, and gave it to the woman. Isella cringed because his beautiful Converse shoes would be muddied. He wiped his shoes against the tires, sat back in the car, and drove back to school.

---

[32] Dummy
[33] My truck was parked here.

She thought about her predicament. "Mom is going to be so pissed!"

It took a while for them to park, and neither one of them said anything. She thanked him and left.

Isella went to two periods. After lunch, she sat with Viddie in silence, ignoring the numerous texts from Rich.

Viddie was unusually quiet. She wore flats today which made her shorter than usual. Viddie was one of the shortest girls in the class, and unlike Isella, she was plump. Her curly hair was cropped short, but her hair was beautiful. Isella often "propped" her friend who didn't always think she was attractive and exaggerated how fat she was. She smirked at Viddie who kept glancing at the phone and Isella texted, *I can't see you until after Christmas. I have to buy groceries, and my damn truck got towed.*

Well, hello to you, my love, he replied.

They went back and forth, him offering to help, but she knew his mom hadn't seen him in a long time and couldn't in good conscience take him away from his ideal parents.

"What's up with you girl?" Viddie asked. "What's *The Boy* want?"

"I'm experiencing drama and don't have time for The Boy." That's all she said before she went to her next class. For some inhumane reason, she had P.E. right after lunch. Most days, she was great at sports, but she was distracted and thinking about Rich and Friendster and the weird Purple Pants man. The old thoughts competed with the cost of getting the truck back and fixing the tire, all thoughts which slammed into her non-existent calm. She served the ball and considered where the truck could be.

"Look lively!" said Coach Ramirez.

She was about to focus, when an excruciating pain on her left breast made her double over.

"Sorry!" said Amanda Barry, "Oh my gosh!"

Coach Ramirez ran to her. "Are you okay?"

Isella hugged herself, doubling over in pain.

"Go get some ice packs!" ordered Coach Ramirez.

"I'm fine." She breathed through her grimace and tried to stand straight up. He held her right elbow, as he had a larger girl help her to the nurse's office. The walk was a few minutes away, but this time, it took her a long time to get there.

"You okay?" the tall freckled girl kept asking.

"Yeah," Isella managed after the eighth query.

When they arrived, the girl babbled what happened, and the nurse dismissed her. The nurse was a dark-haired, wiry woman with a lean face that could cut through steel. Isella had never spoken to her but knew she was tough by reputation. The nurse called in for someone to help, and it was the ever-friendly Ms. Smith, the school secretary. The nurse had Isella remove her shirt and enormous bra.

"Oooh," said the nurse trying to be neutral, "you're going to have quite a bruise. I know it's going to be uncomfortable, but we're going to put some ice on it." The nurse looked through her files. "No allergies to Tylenol?"

Isella shook her head. "I hate these gargantuan breasts."

"Well," said the nurse, "you may hate them a little more for a few days. Keep the ice on for ten minutes at a time, and I'm not trying to be racist, but please don't do any home remedies. Please. If you feel any lumps that won't go away, go see your doctor." The nurse gave her an understanding look. "I used to think I had enormous breasts. My body caught up, more or less."

"Mom has them," said Isella. "It's our curse."

"Well," chimed in the secretary, who had been quiet the whole time, "you can always get a better support bra." They both smiled tight smiles at her, which told Isella that suggestion wouldn't help at all.

Isella kept the ice pack on her throbbing chest, until the full ten minutes were up. She handed her a slip.

The nurse said, "You can study for the rest of P.E. in the library. Keep alternating the ice pack and bring it back when you're done."

"I'll take Coach Ramirez the note," said the secretary.

Isella walked back to the library, but the pain would not let her study. Fourth period would begin soon, but she couldn't wait to find her truck. She still hadn't called her mother and wouldn't until she exhausted her options.

She was scheming, when someone tapped her shoulder.

"Hey." It was the silver-shoed knight.

"Hey Harry," she responded.

He smiled, and she noticed that his eyes were grey.

"So, I called my dad who works for the D.M.V. He made a few calls. Your truck is most likely at Joe's Lot on 6th Avenue; according to Dad, you probably got a $50 ticket for parking it on the side of the road. If the cops were there. Dad says it could be more but getting it out of the lot is going to be $150."

She grimaced at that amount.

He continued and said. "Then, there's the repair, which Joe can do for a small fee."

"Where am I going to get that kind of cash? Christmas will be totally ruined."

"Well," he said, "I know we don't know each other well, but I could loan you the money."

Isella glared at him. "In exchange for what?"

"I know you work at the swap meet. I do too, selling comics. You've never noticed me." He blushed. "I don't think. I know you're good for it."

She paused to think. Isella didn't recall ever seeing him, but she was so focused on making money. The truth is that she wasn't social with the other vendors. In fact, nobody knew her name. Isella just focused on potential buyers or reading when sales were slow.

"Well." She stuttered. "That's awfully generous of you. I can pay you back with interest."

"No," he said. "No need. Just go with me to the dance. I'll be bored to tears, and we can talk about academics. Or Depeche Mode."

Before she could think, she blurted out, "I have a boyfriend. Sort of."

He gave her a quizzical look, and she said, "Fine. I'll go, but I am not making out with you or anything. I'm not a cheater, and I'm only going if he says it's okay. Got it?"

He smiled. "Awesome! I wasn't expecting you to do anything. I know you're not like that. Look, we can go as friends."

Isella expected him to say more, but instead, he walked to his next class, and she meandered to honor's English, the last class before their Academic Decathlon meeting.

ACADEMIC DECATHLON WAS as uneventful that afternoon, as the morning meeting, even with the whole team there. She managed to solve all of the math problems in record time and spent extra time with the C-team. Harry smiled at her, and she smirked back, which elicited some gossip.

Before Harry left, she asked, "Can I have a ride home?"

"Of course, I figured," he said. "Let's go, Champ."

Isella cringed. "Dude, don't call me nicknames or else, I'll walk home."

That was the Isella everyone knew. Hard. Stubborn. She talked to her team but wasn't friends with them. Even when she went to socials, she would stay for an hour and leave.

"I have to get my truck, or Christmas is ruined," she said.

They went to an A.T.M., where Harry pulled out a gold card and took out $200. She took the money and stuffed it her back pocket and sat quietly as Harry used a map app with funny commentary to get to the lot. The app vocalized, *Don't miss your turn, you big dork.* They arrived with both of them laughing despite Isella's stress.

"Just my bad luck," she said. The lot was closed for the holidays. She called the number on a rusty sign and a throaty voice answered. After a few questions, she found out the foreman of the lettuce field had her car towed. She hadn't gotten a ticket, as far as he knew.

"I'll be back Monday, at 7, sorry kiddo. I got people coming in from Oklahoma. Look, I got an old tire that matches yours; yours is shreds. I can give you a discount, $40 for the tire and repair. Merry Christmas." Joe hung up before she could say yes.

Isella cursed out loud.

"Don't worry." Harry adjusted his glasses. "I can drive you around. I don't celebrate Christmas." She looked at him as he pulled out a star of David.

He explained, "We converted a few years back. La'chaim."

"Uh, La'chaim," said Isella. "I watch a lot of Jewish movies. That would be great. I can give you gas money. Plus, I'm avoiding Rich."

"Oh?" he asked perking up.

Isella told him about the distance growing between them. She explained that even though they were going steady, she had been to his house a few times and never for Christmas dinner. The truth was that she was worried his parents would freak out if they found out she was Mexican-American. Rich for his part didn't want his parents meddling in his affairs like they did often with his older siblings, so as far as his parents knew, she was a girl in his former Academic Decathlon team and past debate partner.

"Damn," said Harry, "that's cold."

"Trust me. It's not," she assured. "I mean how would your parents feel if you brought someone like me home?"

"Hey," he said, "we're from a historically underrepresented group! Besides, you're half right. They would disapprove of 50% of you."

She laughed out loud.

"Where to, madam?" he asked.

They went to Don Julio's and struggled to find parking. Luckily, his car was small, and he managed to park illegally along with another group of shoppers.

"Yeah, don't sweat it," she said. "No one's going to tow you here."

The store was crowded, and she had a moment of panic. Maybe all the meat was gone. She rushed to the butcher as Harry maneuvered through the tight shoppers.

She got to the meat counter, Don Julio smiling as though there wasn't a throng of clients. There were twelve people ahead of her, and as she rattled off the 12 days of Christmas in her head, he said, -¿Que hubo güerita?-[34] His large handle-bar moustache pointed up and his kind brown eyes warmed her. Don Julio was uncharacteristically tall with a bald head and round face. He walked away before she could order and pulled out a ten-pound turkey and ten-pound mass of pork from the side of the fridge where he kept goodies for regulars and family. He smiled and asked, "Eh, did I guess right?"

"You saved me!" she said. "You're the best, Don Julio."

Harry came up beside her with a cart. Don Julio scrutinized the boy as a testy uncle might.

"Friend from school," she said and added, "The truck got towed while I was at school. Stupid foreman from the lettuce field. He towed it, so my buddy here is helping me out."

---

[34] What's up blondie?

124

"Sorry, mijita," he said, "on the house!" He gave her a small package of cheese and put a signature $0. "For your mom. Tell her it's a Christmas gift from me."

Isella giggled and took the package. Don Julio waved goodbye and went back to tend the long line.

Harry was having a marvelous time asking questions about products and taking a few things himself, including a jar of jalapeños. When they found the corn husks for tamales, they were done.

He helped her as a brother might putting the groceries into categories.

"You shop for your mom?"

"No," he said, "she died when I was seven."

Isella paled and apologized. "I'm sorry. You said earlier, and I didn't connect the dots."

"It's okay," he said. "My new mom, Sarah, is as good as any mother. Dad married her when I was nine, two years after my mom died. But, I miss Mom."

Isella squeezed his shoulder which made him blush and start to laugh his nerdy laugh.

"Put your stuff on the belt, Harry. I got you."

He tried to object, but she was stubborn. Besides, she had no gas money to offer. Not if she was going to get the gifts for her mom. They made one more stop at the Avon store close to the grocery store.

On the drive home, Harry put on Depeche Mode, and she was surprised she could sing to some of the songs. They were both quiet, and as they neared their gated community, a chill grew through her body. She hadn't told Harry how to get to her house, and she knew for a fact, he wasn't one of her neighbors. *Or was he?*

Every horrible doubt made its way through her brain. She looked at him as sweat began to form on her forehead.

"Where to?" he asked giving her a concerned look.

"Um, turn right," she said. "You can just leave me out front, outside the gate."

"Don't be silly," he insisted. "I can help. That's a lot of stuff you got."

"Nah. You've done so much," she stammered. He was going to press again, but as he neared her house, she almost shouted for joy. Rich was there in a new red car. Brand new.

Rich smiled at her and grew serious when he saw Harry.

Her boyfriend said, "Hey baby."

She got out of the car, and he embraced her giving her a long, drawn-out kiss. Rich whispered, "What's wrong?"

She rolled her eyes towards Harry and said, "Tell you later."

"Harry?" asked Rich, giving him a hard handshake. "How are you, bruh?"

They exchanged pleasantries, but Harry became his awkward self again. For her part, she grabbed the groceries and made two trips carrying overly heavy loads.

"Harry," she said, "I can't thank you enough."

"I'll take you to the lot on Monday," he said. It wasn't a request, and before she could protest, he was gone.

Rich gave her a long look, and she explained the whole sequence of events, as they walked into the house. By the time she was done organizing everything in the refrigerator and kitchen, Rich was upset.

"So," he said running his fingers through his long hair, "you think Harry's a stalker?"

"God," she said exasperated, "I'm not sure. I mean, he is so nice, but something's off."

"Maybe," he said and added, "this dummy figured he had a shot at you. I mean, you are gorgeous. What was it? Prettier than the Virgin Mary." He smirked, followed by an unkind laugh.

She hardened and almost spilled her guts about wanting to break up. She paused and took in all the changes. His hair was longer past his ears, and he had grown slimmer, but he still had that kindness in his eyes.

"So," she hedged and blurted out, "are you seeing anyone else?"

Rich took a step back. "No. Why do you think that?"

"You just," she said, "you seem different." She sat on the stool, but before she could explain he wrapped his arms around her and kissed her.

"I'm not seeing anyone," he said. "Are you?"

"Are you serious? I don't even have time to pee. I spend most of my time trying to make ends meet, and this whole truck thing's almost ruined Christmas." Isella began to tear up and despite her toughness, began to cry.

In the movies, there's a series of events where the boy drags the girl to the bedroom. For Isella, the sequence of events was muddled and slow. By the time, they got to her bedroom, which is not where she wanted to be, they were on her bed, with Rich tracing his hand up her left leg.

She separated herself from him and grew tense. "I don't want to—"

"It's okay," he said stiffening.

She thought, *Was he annoyed?*

"We don't have to do anything you don't want to."

He kissed her again tight, removing her Hello Kitty underwear, as though he were practiced. He had never done that before, but now he was precise.

He pressed against her, and she was about to tell him to stop, but in that moment, he massaged her breast causing her to yelp.

"Stop! Please stop!"

Rich kept pressing, and she pushed him away as hard as she could.

"What's wrong?" he asked growing upset.

"I forgot to tell you the best part of my day." She sighed, showing the bruise. She disentangled herself and went to the kitchen to get ice and Tylenol. Her bruise started to ache again but not as bad as before. She wanted to text Viddie because he was still in her room, not that she would be supportive. Isella debated all options, but she couldn't do it.

She walked back holding a compress to her chest. Rich was lying in her bed under the covers with a large stuffed animal over his face.

"Are you crying?" she asked and started teasing him.

"No," he said, "come here."

She shook her head. "No. I think you should go. Mom will kill me."

"We'll just cuddle."

She got into bed as images of taking Viddie to the clinic raced through her head. "I had to take Viddie to the clinic to get tested a few months ago."

He gave her a worried look. "Is she okay?" He got up and began to stroke her back. "Come back."

"No, please go before I get in trouble," she said.

Rich got out of bed and towered over her. "I thought you wanted this. She told me you wanted to give me this awesome present, and I thought . . ."

Isella pushed him away. "That skank! I don't want that. I don't want to, and you said you would wait." She pressed the compress to her breast again.

He was about to leave in a huff, but she handed him the large box.

Rich said, "Fine. I'll see you later, but I hope you'll figure out what it is you want." He took the gift.

She sat at the edge of the bed and was poised between calling Rich back and texting Viddie a nasty gram. Instead she got on the Kanji and watched Friendster's video one more time. A thought began to emerge like when she solved puzzles. She watched the video a couple of times and paused it as she scanned the laundry pile. There was a black t-shirt and the background was blurry, but something had been tugging at her memory all morning. She watched the video a few times pausing at different frames, and sure enough, there was a silver Converse.

He sent her another friend request, and she accepted.

"Cut the crap, Harry," she said through her headset. She was going to say more, but he went offline.

VIDDIE TEXTED HER THE NEXT DAY, but Isella needed to think. Besides, she was angry at her. It was 9:00 a.m., and she waited for Rich. Against her better judgement, she put on her Christmas dress ahead of schedule and her gold flats. He came to her front door with a large poinsettia and a bottle of cider.

"Oh, you look sexy, but I thought we were cooking so." He looked at his old sneakers and torn jeans.

"That's okay." She gave him a long kiss and kicked herself. *What was she doing?* Rich put the poinsettia on a glass coffee table in the living room and put the cider into the refrigerator.

When she came back out, she was wearing grey shorts and a white t-shirt with no bra because her chest felt better without it. Isella wasn't used to cooking with anyone, but he was intent on helping out.

"Won't your mom get mad?" she asked.

He shook his head. "I told her I was going Christmas shopping."

He explained that he was going shopping for his dad who was picky, but he wanted to spend as much time as possible with her. Besides, he had exciting news.

She waited, as he hesitated and said, "I'm going abroad."

"What?" she asked.

"I get to go to Japan to learn about robotics, and I can't pass this up. I'm not breaking up with you. It's just for a semester. Besides, I was hoping we'd grow closer together."

Closer together? she wondered what that meant. She held her breath. Isella was conflicted. On the one hand, she wasn't sure what they were doing together anymore. On the other hand, now that he was in front of her, she didn't want to break up.

"I don't want to end things either," she said, "but I won't be pressured, Rich. You're not getting a farewell gift before you go off to kill Godzilla or eat exotic sushi."

He kissed her forehead. "Racist much?"

She laughed. "Hey, maybe you could find out who the 97 Clan is. I think they're third graders."

He hugged her tight and wouldn't let go. Isella began to grow uncomfortable and said, "I'm on a schedule." They began the long process of making tamales. First, she bossed him to get a large pot of water boiling with the pork mass inside. It was ten pounds of pure pork; the best Don Julio could provide with little to no fat. She grew upset when she determined carrying heavy things flared up her injured breast.

"I hate my chest," she said between painful breaths.

"I don't," he said smiling at her as he sipped a Coke and kept staring at her chest.

"Shut up."

When the pork was done boiling, Rich put it in a large aluminum pan, so it could cool off. Between steps, he kept leaning into her, sometimes stealing a kiss. He stopped annoying her, when he helped her pour hot broth into the corn meal for the tamale dough.

Between stolen affection and complicated tasks, Rich explained what a great opportunity it would be to study robotics. He had impressed some visiting professors during a poster presentation at a conference, and even though he was Freshman, they had taken a liking to him.

"Won't your mom freak with you being so far away?"

He nodded his head. "Dad convinced her."

He observed with great interest as she mixed the dough. He asked her, "Isn't that hot?" He watched with fascination. Rich didn't miss her grimaces.

"Let me have a try."

"Ah," she said, "it's almost done. No point in you getting your hands dirty. You can help me shred the pork."

He snuck up behind her and held her there.

"Okay, I need to finish," she said.

His face stiffened, and when he didn't listen to her, she moved away.

He eyed the pork nervously. "Uh, is there something else I can do besides shredding the pork?"

She showed him how to rinse the corn husks in hot water making sure to take out any corn threads or dirt. She explained, "It's a huge cultural faux pas if you find corn hairs in the tamales."

He saluted understanding the importance of his task.

"You know," he added, "you can come visit me. I mean, not just in Japan. I can pay, plus, you can visit the college."

"I'll never be able to pay you back, but thanks," she said.

131

"You wouldn't have to." He turned to look at her from the sink. "I miss you. I know I've been a dweeb, but I miss you." Isella grew tense, and he closed in again. He held her so tight her chest began to hurt.

Her mother walked into the kitchen. "Hey Rich. What are you doing here?" He stopped what he was doing and gave her mom a tremendous hug.

He said, "Helping this one out. She got injured in P.E. yesterday."

Her mother gave her a concerned look.

"It's nothing, just a big bruise," Isella assured.

"Turn around," her mother told Rich as she looked under Isella's shirt. "Oh honey."

"It's no big, Mom." She looked away. There was no point in waiting to give her the terrible news. She looked at Rich and back to her Mom.

Her mother stared as Isella mouthed *It's okay.* By the look on her mom's face, she knew her mom was expecting some major confession. Instead, Isella explained about the flat tire and the truck.

Her mother sat on the same stool Isella had plummeted into the previous night. "How much?"

"$190, but I borrowed money from a classmate, and he is not charging interest. I offered."

"I bet he's not," said Rich growing irritated. "I'll pay him. You don't have to pay me or do at your own pace. I know how prideful you Latinas are."

Isella's mother laughed. "Learn that at M.I.T.?" Before Isella could object, her mother began to help, which pretty much consisted of her cleaning after their messes. She only had a short time for lunch. Before departing, her mother said, "Don't worry. I can get the money. Besides. I'm expecting a bonus."

When she was done wiping down the counters, she said, "I will see you later. I'm only working four more hours, okay?"

Isella smiled. "What?"

"Pulled some favors."

It was almost noon, and Rich was a mess. He had dough on his cheek and forehead. They talked for a while longer before he left. He tried kissing her once more, but she flinched. Still, he pressed against her and kept kissing.

She moaned but wanted him to stop. Rich misunderstood her response and started running his fingers up her right leg. She began to breath heavily, as he began to take off her shorts.

"No," she said, "The kitchen is gross."

"Well, let's go to your bedroom."

This time, time ran fast. She began to panic as he lifted her up and carried her to the bed.

"Listen, I can't go all the way," she insisted.

He ignored her as he took her shorts and underwear off. He kissed her without letting her protest. The heat was radiating up her body.

Richard would not listen, and he ran his finger rhythmically saying, "It's all right."

But it wasn't all right because Rich had never been that aggressive or schooled about girls.

He took a break to breathe, and Isella said, "We should stop." A sudden image of her father made her grow cold. She tried pushing him away, but he started unzipping his pants. Isella had enough.

She slapped him, hard enough to make him slow down.

"I said stop."

He scoffed, rubbing his left cheek, and said, "Maybe this will soften you up." He threw a small box on her bed.

Rich pulled his pants up and left. He didn't wish her Merry Christmas.

Isella rested there for a while, until her heart stopped hammering. Part of her felt like a jerk and shouldn't have let things get so far. The other part had horrible visions of her being a single mother in a worse position than she was in now. She got up, put on her panties and shorts, and went back to work.

When the tamales were boiling, she brought them down to a simmer and proceeded with the turkey. Her precise cooking style had her focus on the tasks at hand. She didn't want to think about Rich or the flat tire or Harry or that weird Purple Pants Freak.

She analyzed the turkey.

"I wish I had brined you."

This was the first time she roasted a turkey this way, without marinating it for three days. Don Julio had been an absolute prince and thawed out the bird. She melted butter and wine together and put seasoning in the mixture. To add some flair, she injected the creature in the legs and breast, using a large cooking syringe and planned to put turkey to roast upside down.

"I forgot the roasting bag," she said to no one, but then, had the idea of putting it into a paper bag. She thought better of it, and just put the turkey on the baking sheet as she planned. She crammed an apple where the stuffing should have been. Her mother was not a fan of stuffing and neither was she. She had a radical idea and sliced some thick apples, putting them on top of the bird and around the sides as a shield. Next, she wrapped the turkey in aluminum foil keeping most of the apples in place, which would keep the bird moist, and protected from being burned.

Once the bird was in the oven, she proceeded to make a variety of vegetable dishes. Her favorite were rosemary carrots.

Isella also loved cranberry sauce, and she boiled two fresh bags in orange juice and cinnamon. That smell centered her into contentment. Before long, the berries began to crack, and she stirred the sugar quickly and set them aside.

When she was done making all the side dishes, she opted to wait to make the pies for later. In fact, she was getting more tired than usual. That encounter with Rich had drained her. It was 5:00 p.m., and Viddie had texted her ten times. She finally responded by saying, *The Boy. He was super sweet and respectful.* That was an absolute lie. Rich didn't send her text messages.

Viddie sent a disappointed kitty emoji. Isella would have to confront her about her big mouth, her big mouth that had urged Rich to push Isella's boundaries. Instead, she decided to call Viddie and settle things.

"Hey," said Viddie, "give me all the details."

"No," Isella said, "look, he came here thinking I wanted to put out. He went too far, but I don't *want* to go all the way, okay? So, stop meddling. I almost broke up with him because of you!"

Before Viddie could object and make excuses, Isella said, "I'm sorry about what happened to you, but you have to stop getting into my love life. I'll give it up when I want. Because I want to. You can tell him that."

Viddie tried to get defensive.

"Don't even try it. He told me what you said." She hung up.

In their long years of friendship, she hadn't ever hung up on Viddie, but Viddie had never betrayed her like that either. They were even.

Isella decided to take a bath and soothe the pain on her chest. One of the best features of the house was a large bathtub her mother always coveted. It was more like a hot tub, made for two. She quickly put on her bathrobe and went to her mother's room. The tub was immaculate, unused for weeks.

She let the water rise as she sprinkled in bath salts and bubbles. Isella inspected the bath salts. They were rich with lavender scent.

"I didn't get these for you," she said and wondered who had.

Isella eased into the tub and soaked her feet, which she discovered were aching. Her phone was set against a large shampoo bottle streaming a show about witches and teenage angst. She thought long and hard about Rich. She asked herself, "Would I have kept going?" Isella wasn't sure, but she was convinced they would have been ruined. Stupid Viddie. She tried to put these thoughts aside.

Her eyes grew heavier, and she almost leaped out of the tub when she saw the Purple Prankster hovering over her, but it was just the trick of her eyes. She grew comfortable again, and before long, she began to slither below the warm water.

"ISELLA!" THE SCREAM WOKE her from a happy dream of eating sushi in Tokyo with Rich. Later, in the dream, they found the clan of kids living on the streets in an abandoned basement, playing on a stolen Kanji. She was about to hand them a box of food, when her mother's cries woke her.

She was standing over her with a man she didn't recognize. "Sweetie!"

Isella woke up, cold and naked on the bathroom floor, her chest in terrible pain.

"What happened?" asked her mother checking her.

"I don't know."

The man walked out of the bathroom.

Isella explained, "I was taking a bath, and I must have been tired. I'm fine mom."

She sat up and put on her robe, so her friend checked her.

He said, "Pulse is fine. I think she's fine. She is bruised on the center of her chest and breast, but not fractured, I don't think. Someone did C.P.R."

Isella looked at the Indian man. He introduced himself as Dr. Pakar, the dermatologist.

"I invited him to dinner," said her mom.

"Ah," she said ignoring her near-death experience and pain. "We need to make pies." Her mother gave her an exasperated look, but she also knew how stubborn Isella could be.

"If you feel off," said her mother, "we go to the E.R., understood?"

Isella nodded her head. She took one last look at the bathroom floor, and she was sure there was sporadic glitter on it and in the small pools of water. She shook her head. In her room, Isella took off her robe and stared at her chest. There were fingerprints there.

"Hmm," she said to herself, "who pulled you out of the tub? Was it Harry?"

When she got to the kitchen, she was wearing her Christmas dress and gold shoes again. She had wrapped the two lipsticks in gold and green paper and set them under the tree.

Isella went to bake the pies and was surprised Dr. Pakar was already starting on the dough. She laughed when she saw him wearing the apron of La Virgen de Guadalupe. He stepped aside.

"I have five younger brothers and a busy mum." He smiled. The man was handsome with thick curls and perfect features. No wonder her mother was smitten.

"You married?" Isella asked as her mother protested.

"Widowed, four years later divorced," he answered. "No kids."

"Pakar an Indian name?" she prodded.

"British."

She wanted to ask more, but he didn't want to ruin the holiday any more than she had. She worked the crust's dough and paced herself on the strawberries. Isella had perfected her pie-filling recipe over the years, so much that she made extra for the crepes she would be cooking tomorrow.

"Your mom says you got a flat," he said. She explained All the troubles, highlighting the foreman who had her car towed. He listened so well, she told him about her problem with Harry but neglected to talk about Rich.

"What do you think?" she asked.

He thought for a while. "You are certain it was the same Converse?"

"You can't be too careful, Izzie," said her Mom.

"Mom," she almost shouted, "don't call me that."

Dr. Pakar laughed. "I like it."

"No," said Isella and added. "What do we call you? Dr. Pakar? Bit pompous, no?"

"Izzie!" protested her mom.

"Yes, rather elitist," he agreed and chuckled. "Adam, please."

Isella nodded. "We're all just surviving the American Dream."

"Aren't we, just?" He smiled at her and dipped his finger into the strawberries. The nod of approval won her over a bit more.

He advised, "I think you should ask him point blank. The boy clearly has a crush on you, I think. But your mum is right. I wouldn't do it alone."

"Ah," she said, "Viddie and I aren't on great terms. Don't ask why Mom. Girl trouble."

Dinner that evening was more festive than usual. Dr. Pakar who grew up in England brought crackers and hats. The crackers were just like she had seen on T.V., cylinders made out of crepe paper with bad jokes inside. He was a thoughtful man, and he made sure to dote over her mother without being sappy. The fact that she couldn't cook had not escaped him, but he complemented her table decorations and attention to detail. Her mother had put on a rich velvet crimson table cloth on the small dining room table for four and gold napkins with Christmas rings. The plates had been Isella's find at the swap meet, three complete white porcelain sets. The serving plates and platters were mismatched, but that didn't bother Adam

"Shoot," said Isella, "I forgot to make salsa."

"Don't bother! Everything is perfect."

Still, Isella couldn't let it go. "It will only take a moment."

She took the blender from the cabinet and from the vegetable basket, three raw tomatoes, half an onion, and her own garden red peppers, a crop that vexed her nosy neighbors because she wasn't planting flowers. She added garlic and salt and pepper. She started the blender and looked out the window. Just then, she saw Harry's car parked at a distance, two blocks away. He was parked in front of the retired lawyer's house.

Was he stalking her? she wondered. He was standing outside the car poised as if stuck between motion. The blender stopped, and she absentmindedly dipped her finger in it and took a taste.

"That smells divine," said Adam. He looked out the window in the direction where she looked.

"It's Harry," she said growing angry. "You got my back?" Before he could answer, she stormed out of the front door.

Her mother called out to her, but she wouldn't be stopped.

She marched out to his car and reached him before she could formulate what she would say.

She reached him within minutes. "Are you stalking me?"

"What?" he said. He was holding a green Christmas bag. "What? No. My parents are having dinner here."

"Tell the truth," she said getting closer to him. "You're Friendster!"

A tall blonde woman called from the house. "Is everything all right, Harry?"

"Fine Mom. She's on the decathlon team, too," he answered barely audible. He was turning bright red.

"Tell the truth, Harry, so help me." Before he could answer she went on, "I almost drowned in the tub today, and I remember you took that C.P.R. class with me. Did you save me?"

"Oh man, are you okay?" he asked.

"Don't change the subject! Are you him or not?" Isella jabbed him on the chest, punctuating every syllable, and thought to do worse.

By this point his father had also come out, an older version of Harry wearing a dark brown suit. The vixen emerged in a white lacy dress.

"Hey, a girl is talking to Harry!" she said.

Harry looked miserable and stared at the gift unsure what to do. He gulped audibly. "Yes."

Without thinking, she slapped him, which brought a simultaneous loud gasp from his mother and a laugh from his sister. A whistle from his father. She stormed away.

"Go after her." She heard his father advise.

"Don't even try it!" she hollered. She turned back. "I don't ever want to talk to you again, you weirdo!"

140

"Best Christmas ever, and we're Jewish!" said his sweet sister as Isella reached her house.

Adam and her mother rushed to the table, pretending not to have seen all the drama unfold from the kitchen window.

Isella went to her room, lay on her bed, and screamed into her pillow. She lay there for twenty minutes before her mother cajoled her back to the table.

"Come on, we haven't had a guest in forever," she said. "Let me take a look at that hand."

Isella emerged from her room and gave Adam a fixed look. "I'm not a drama queen, in case you're wondering."

He understood and motioned for her to sit. She explained everything that happened.

"I was right." She put her head in her hands. "Now, I have to pay him back his money."

"Don't worry," said her mother. "I got that bonus. Look, I don't want to excuse his lying or behavior, but you can be well, intimidating."

Glaring at her mother, Isella put half the pie piece in her mouth.

"She has a right to assert herself," defended Adam. "Good for standing up for yourself, but I do think you should let him explain. After all, he seems to have friends here, just down the street." He made a gesture towards the neighbors.

"Yeah," she said, "I thought of that." Isella considered that point, as her mother poured three glasses of sherry and gave her a small glass. She gave her mother a quizzical look.

Her mother said, "I think you could use a small drink."

Isella smiled and took a small sip. They cheered, and the doorbell rang. Her mother went to open the door, and Viddie was standing there. Her eyes were red, and her mouth caught between being a slit and a frown.

"What's wrong?" She came in holding a large gift and the bag Harry had been carrying.

"I've been a jerk." She rushed to Isella and babbled an apology.

"Stop, stop. I forgive you."

"This was on your doorstep with a note," she said holding up the bag.

Isella stared at them for so long, her mother put both gifts under the tree.

"Oh." Viddie began to cry. "You *are* mad at me! You don't want my present."

"No." Isella gave hear a heartfelt hug and ushered her towards the table. They all sat and eased back into the spirit of the dinner. Dr. Pakar put his hat back.

Viddie grabbed a tortilla and dunked it in the hot sauce. She looked over to Dr. Pakar. "Who are you?"

Isella introduced them, "This is Dr. Pakar, Mom's co-worker," and arched her eyebrows in a meaningful way, "and this is Viddie, my best friend since second grade."

Adam rose up and shook her hand.

"What did you make? I'm starving. Mom made a disgusting roast and runny potatoes, and I couldn't eat a bite I was so worried. She got tired of my moping and told me to come over."

Without being asked, her mother put a plate together.

Between large chews, Viddie asked, "So, you slapped him? In front of his family You know his dad's a lawyer, right? Damn, these tamales are awesome!"

Isella was still justified by her anger. "He said his dad worked for the D.M.V."

"You know," said Viddie, "and I'm not trying to stick my nose in your love affairs, I think he is a nice guy. He doesn't give me the weirdo psycho vibe. He's just so shy and awkward. He know you have a man?" She paused. "You do have a man, right?"

"Yes," said Isella, "definitely, but I think we're done."

"Can I have a glass of that?" asked Viddie.

"Your mom let you drink?" they all asked in unison. She shook her head.

"I've had enough," said Isella giving the glass to her mom who took it with gratitude.

Without pausing, Viddie asked, "Can I spend the night? I already asked my mom. My brother's entire family drove down from Washington, without telling anyone. 'Surprise!' They've invaded my room, and those kids are so annoying! They won't get off my Kanji."

"Sure," said Isella. "You can stay as long as you want. Besides, I almost died today." When she said it out loud, she realized that was the truth.

Her mother gave her a concerned look. "Maybe you should go to the hospital."

"Mom, I just ate a full plate and ate two pieces of pie. I'm fine."

"Who pulled you out of the tub?" asked Viddie.

Isella shrugged her shoulders, but she had her suspicions. Viddie looked at her face and asked, "What's wrong?"

She struggled with what she was going to say or to say anything at all. Without censoring, she explained what happened with Rich. Her mother shook her head, and Adam asked, "You asked him to stop? I don't think his conduct is acceptable. At all."

Viddie sucked in hard. "It's my fault. I told him you were ready."

'That doesn't matter!" said her mother.

That set a morose tone to the following gift exchange. Before it was time to exchange presents, Isella went to her room and wrapped a favorite hardcover for Adam. It was a collection of her favorite mystery short stories. She wrapped it in the last silver paper and topped it with a blue bow.

He was surprised when she handed him a gift, and she was too when she got something almost equal. She supposed he and her mother talked about her literary tastes.

Isella held the pouch from Rich. She opened it, and Viddie gasped. It was a small box, like one that held an expensive ring.

"Oh, zip it, Viddie." But Isella could tell all eyes were on her. Without asking, Viddie began to record her reaction on her phone.

She opened it with great care. It was perfect. A white gold ring with a sapphire, one for each year they had been dating. There was a small note. *I promise to always be yours, but I hope you give me the best gift of all, so you can be mine. Love, Rich.* Isella was speechless and put it on the ring finger of her right hand, and just as quickly took it off and put it back in the box. Her blood froze as she made a decision, once and for all, but she would wait until they were done opening gifts. She wasn't going to ruin anymore of their evening.

"Well," said Viddie, "he just loved the video I posted."

"Viddie!" Isella shot her a look. She stared at the green bag from Harry. When Viddie stopped videoing, to open her gift, she almost fell out of her seat.

Viddie exclaimed, "I love them!" Isella had bought Viddie a shirt from her favorite comic shop and gotten her an accessory to throw grenades, a Kanji glove for her left hand. Isella had saved for it for over six months, and that is one of the reasons she was so broke.

"All I got you was this stupid spray bottle!" she said.

"I don't care," said Isella. She took one more glance at the offensive green bag, and she opened it. It contained a long letter, which she didn't wait to read. It was an apology where he admitted to being Friendster17 and having a crush on her for the longest time. He detailed the times he tried to talk to her but had been ignored or unseen by her, but he said more than anything, he just wanted to be friends.

"Boo hoo," Isella muttered. She looked in the bag and paused. It was the first graphic novel by Inia Beginning. Signed. She gasped in surprise. But, thought back and remembered her Academic Decathlon speech; she had referenced the author. Plus, she always carried a copy of the author's latest book.

Isella read the letter one more time and handed it to Viddie who nodded her head in appreciation, but Viddie said, "He's still a major loser."

It made the rounds even to Adam who said, "Sounds like a sensitive boy, but not crazy. I think."

THAT NIGHT, ISELLA HAD A NIGHTMARE. She dreamt she was at a pool. Her father was still around but chatting with a couple of college girls. Isella couldn't have been more than four years old, but she could swim. Somehow, she grew bold and began to wade out to the deep end, while her father continued to flirt.

Isella remembered one of the girls removed something from his face with her slim fingers. She began to grow jealous and was going to tell her Mommy. In an instant, a sharp pain in her left leg made her gasp. She sunk as she flailed calling for her dad, but he did not come. She sank almost to the bottom of the pool, when a pair of strong arms floated her upwards. Her vision began to grow dark, as a mist of white hairs floated past her eyes, and she rose above the water.

Her father jumped into the pool and took her out. One of the college students pressed on her chest and breathed in her mouth. The force was unbearable, but before long, she coughed water, some of it shooting up her nose. When the ambulance took her to the hospital, she was fine.

ISELLA WOKE WITH A START and headed for the kitchen. She was careful not to wake Viddie who snored like an indelicate horse. The clock on the stove read 1:00 a.m. Isella got a mug and was about to make tea, when Dr. Pakar walked in. There was an awkward pause.

"Would you like some tea?"

He nodded as her mother came after him.

They didn't say anything for a while, but Isella said, "Mom, did I almost drown when I was little?"

Her mother blanched. She sat heavily at the counter. "That was the day I decided to become a nurse." Her mother explained that her father had been preoccupied, talking to people as usual. It wasn't the first time, but this time he was getting drunk. She had been in their hotel room with a terrible migraine, which she never forgave herself for.

"That was the moment I knew," she said tearing up. "He wasn't meant to be a father."

"Do you know who pulled me out?"

"He did," she answered, "after you almost drowned." Adam put his arm around her mom's shoulder.

Isella looked at the pair of them. They looked great together, and something about Adam felt like home. Isella said, "You know, I hope I see you more often." She left with her cup of tea and was going to go back to her room, when she looked out of the window, and was surprised to see Harry's car still there.

She took a sip from her tea. It was hot, so she put the mug down and made another rash decision. She was wearing thick warm pajamas and slippers. Without losing her courage, she walked out and was about to go ring the doorbell when she noticed he was sitting in the car talking to his sister.

Isella waved to him, and he got out as though there were a zombie in the car.

Before she could say anything, he went into an eloquent apology. Isella went up to him and put her fingers on his mouth. "Look, you don't have to apologize anymore."

"Kiss her!" said his high-pitched sister.

"Is she drunk?" asked Isella.

"Maybe."

"I'm sorry," she said, "and no, I'm not going to kiss you or date you. I will go to the dance, but just as friends. For now. Here."

She handed him the money. "Clean slate, me and you. Sound good?"

He smiled a sheepish smile. "Yeah."

"Oh," she said, "Viddie's going to be hanging out with us."

"Yeah sure!"

"Kiss her, you dolt!" repeated the voice from inside his car.

Isella paused. "You didn't pull me out of the tub?"
He shook his head. "I was waiting for the gift I overnighted."

She walked away laughing and went home feeling better than she had in a long time. For most of her youth, she had been so independent, and she had never been alone. Not really. Isella looked at the top of her roof and swore the Paunchy Purple man was there. She stared and looked back to see if Harry could see him, but when she turned around, the man was gone.

Pausing, she stared at the phone in her hand. She called Rich and was surprised a girl answered. "Is Rich there?"

"Hey, gorgeous." He said laughing.

"Who is that?"

"No one," he said, and she was sure there was an angry feminine protest in the background.

"I got your message," she said. "And I wish I could do this in person, but I'm not putting out for you just because you gave me some fancy ring or because you're going away."

He laughed dismissing her. "Of course, not. I mean, I've only been waiting for years." He took a drink of something.

"I'll give you your ring back," she said beginning to tear up.

"Don't bother." He made an exasperated sound. Rich said, "Look, I get it. You want to wait, and I can't."

She choked a sob. "Well, there's not point, then."

He waited a minute. "Yeah I guess not." With that, she began to cry in earnest and walked home hoping to see the Purple Pants man.

THE NEXT MORNING, she woke up and stared at her ring for a long time. She picked up her phone and called him.

"Hello." Harry was groggy.

"You want to come over for breakfast? Around 8? I'm making crepes."

"Sure," he said beginning that goofy laugh.

"Bring your sister, if you can wake her up."

"Pretend I'm not here," said Viddie under the covers.

They talked for a few more minutes as the sun was coming up, and she invited him to come over for a walk.

"On my way," he said.

"Come on, Vid, let's see the sunrise before we start killing zombies. We'll take turns."

"Oh my God! Did you call The Boy over?"

Isella smiled and got up. "Not exactly." She put on a pair of shorts and a man's medium t-shirt. Viddie was still snuggled in the bed. She mumbled, "I'll be there in a bit." Which meant she needed time to get up.

Isella wasn't startled when she saw them kissing at the table, but she stood there and took it all in. She walked away without disturbing them and made her friend get dressed.

Viddie and Isella left and went for a much-needed walk.

"We spend too much time on the damned Kanji." Decided Isella.

"Yeah, I know."

Isella paused and looked at her friend. "Promise you won't think I'm crazy." She told her about the man in the purple outfit. When she told her about almost drowning at four, Viddie cursed her dad, but for once, Viddie had no snarky response about this person.

"Maybe," she said, "He's your guardian angel." Isella told her about the breakup, which left Viddie open-mouthed.

"It's not your fault Vid," she said. "We were done way before he started getting pushy." Viddie didn't understand, but she knew better than to press. She also knew better than to judge when she realized Harry was coming over.

"So, you have an angel and a new boy?"

"Yes and no," she said, "I have two new friends, but don't get jealous. You're still my best friend."

The gate to the desert was a few yards away, and as they left, Isella looked at the path to their house. On the way to her front door, there was sporadic glitter, which could have been from Christmas decorations, but she knew.

She walked arm in arm with her best friend, feeling secure and protected with the knowledge that come what may, she would never be alone.

Acknowledgements:
¡Muchas Gracias, Todos!

Un gran abrazo y beso to my amazing husband Aaron, my supportive children Antonio and Simona. I need to thank my *carnalita*, Diana, who reads all my work. Ignacio *muchas gracias,* my barrio brother, for your baseball expertise that gave "Unforgivable" street cred. Thank you all who have been reading my drafts and giving me priceless advice, Hector Cruz, Eddie Hartshorn, Todd Heldt, and Mark Kodama, all amazing authors you should read. Support team, you all know who you are, and there are not enough words to express my appreciation. Monique Landsberger deserves a huge gratitude for her editing and copy-editing expertise. I have not forgotten you readers—*muchísimas gracias* for supporting my creations. Finally, a special thank you to my *'Ama* and *'Apa*, whose sacrifices made this amazing writing life possible.

About the Author

MARIA J. ESTRADA is an English college professor of Composition, Literature, and her favorite, Creative Writing. She grew up in the desert outside of Yuma, Arizona in the real *Barrio de Los Locos*, a barrio comprised of new Mexican immigrants and first-generation Chicanos. Drawing from this setting and experiences, she writes like a *loca* every minute she can—all while magically balancing her work and family obligations. She lives in Chicago's south side with her wonderful husband, two remarkable children, and two mischievous cats. You can learn more about her other books and writing happenings at barrioblues.com.

BOOKS BY MARIA J. ESTRADA

ZOMBIES IN THE BARRIO SERIES

The Long Walk

LA BRUJA DEL BARRIO LOCO SERIES

La Bruja in the Orchard
La Bruja del Barrio Loco

Wolf Trek

Zona 5

One Last Favor . . .

If you enjoyed this or any other works by me, follow me on Goodreads!

You can also gift me a short review on Amazon.

Thank you, Readers! I am honored by your support.

-M. Estrada

43124305R00086

Made in the USA
San Bernardino, CA
12 July 2019